"Do You?"

"Do I what?" she snapped, frowning.

"Eat crackers in bed?"

Blythe squeezed her eyes shut and prayed for deliverance. "It's no concern of yours whether I do or not."

Patrick only smiled. For the first time in all their years of competition, Blythe felt she was about to suffer a resounding defeat.

"Patrick, why are you doing this to me? You must realize that last night should never have happened," she said, near desperation. "We're like oil and water, an irresistible force and an immovable object. If you and I were the last man and woman on earth, we still wouldn't be right for each other."

"We've always been right for each other," Patrick found himself saying. "We were just too stubborn to admit it."

Dear Reader,

Welcome to Silhouette! Our goal is to give you hours of unbeatable reading pleasure, and we hope you'll enjoy each month's six new Silhouette Desires. These sensual, provocative love stories are both believable and compelling—sometimes they're poignant, sometimes humorous, but always enjoyable.

Indulge yourself. Experience all the passion and excitement of falling in love along with our heroine as she meets the irresistible man of her dreams and together they overcome all obstacles in the path to a happy ending.

If this is your first Desire, I hope it'll be the first of many. If you're already a Silhouette Desire reader, thanks for your support! Look for some of your favorite authors in the coming months: Stephanie James, Diana Palmer, Dixie Browning, Ann Major and Doreen Owens Malek, to name just a few.

Happy reading!

Isabel Swift
Senior Editor

SDRL-7/85

Joy

JANET JOYCE
Courting Trouble

Silhouette Desire
Published by Silhouette Books New York
America's Publisher of Contemporary Romance

SILHOUETTE BOOKS
300 East 42nd St., New York, N.Y. 10017

Copyright © 1986 by Janet Bieber and Joyce Thies

ISBN: 0-373-05313-4

First Silhouette Books printing November 1986

America's Publisher of Contemporary Romance

Printed in the U.S.A.

Books by Janet Joyce

Silhouette Desire

Winter Lady #53
Man of the House #71
Man of Glory #98
Controlling Interest #116
Run to Gold #140
Rare Breed #168
Out of the Shadows #199
Out of this World #259
Courting Trouble #313

Silhouette Romance

Permanent Fixture #287

JANET JOYCE

resides in Ohio and is happily married to the man who swept her off her feet as a college coed; she admits that her own romance is what prompted her writing career. She and her family like camping, traveling and are avid fans of college football. She is an accomplished pianist, enjoys composing her own lyrics and reads voraciously, especially the romances that she loves.

One
———

"Mr. McBride, this is my third and final warning," Judge Cramer announced. "The Department of Social Welfare is not on trial here, nor is Miss Baker appearing in an official capacity. In that regard, you will stop this line of questioning or be held in contempt."

Patrick McBride clenched his fists in frustration. In order for his client, Sheena Wynbush, to win her case he had to show that by placing her three children in foster homes, she was not a neglectful parent, but had only been doing what was best for their welfare. Of course, opposing counsel had made it seem as if the nineteen-year-old mother of three was unfit, but Patrick knew different. Sheena Wynbush was the victim of a system that paid more to a stranger for child care than it did to the natural mother.

No matter what the consequences, Patrick had to try one more time to show the court that his client shouldn't lose custody of her children to the state. It was true that Madelaine Baker, Sheena's social worker, wasn't present as a representative of the welfare department, but she was the only witness who could prove Sheena's case. Unfortunately, the woman had been on the defensive since taking the stand and about as forthcoming as a clam.

"With all due respect, Your Honor, I see no reason Miss Baker shouldn't respond to the charge of being cruelly remiss in her responsibilities as a social worker. By refusing to inform the court of the inconsistencies in the law under which my client had no choice but to place her children in foster care, she is obstructing justice."

"I repeat, Mr. McBride. The witness is not on trial here."

Patrick was beginning to believe that neither Baker nor the judge hearing the case had one ounce of human feeling. Given his estimation of the judge's personality, this came as no surprise, but Patrick refused to allow his client to become a martyr to such a gross miscarriage of justice. If he was fined for contempt, so be it. It would be well worth it.

His green eyes fired with determination, Patrick faced the bench. "Your Honor, I must protest. You are preventing me from bringing out the facts in this case. In my opinion the welfare department may not be on trial here, but it certainly should be, and Miss Baker's refusal to answer my questions is proof of its guilt."

Turning away from the judge, he pointed at his reluctant witness. "Miss Baker knows damned well that my client is being forced to pay for the inequities of an unfair system and that's the real crime!"

Aware of the risk, he nevertheless took it and again faced the bench. Holding the judge's eyes with his own, he challenged, "A crime *you* will be upholding, Your Honor, if you disallow this line of questioning."

"Is that an attempt to influence my judgment, Mr. McBride?" Judge Cramer inquired with absolute calm.

Patrick was incensed by the judge's lack of response to his challenge, and frustration got the best of him. "Dammit, Your Honor, upholding justice is your duty. I strongly urge you to do so."

A collective gasp rose from the gallery. A heavy gavel hit wood.

"Very well, Mr. McBride," the judge said sternly. "For continued disobedience to my orders, disrespect to this court, and intent to influence my judgment, you are hereby found in contempt. Your remarks have besmirched the dignity of this court and my judicial office. Therefore, you are fined fifty dollars and will be remanded into custody until such time as you are prepared to apologize. Bailiff, please escort Mr. McBride downstairs."

The gavel struck once more, but this time with considerably less force. "This court will be in recess for twenty minutes or however long is necessary for defense counsel to purge himself of his disgraceful conduct."

"And I thought Patrick McBride had been blessed with a fine old Irish temper."

At the sound of her secretary's voice, Judge Blythe Cramer took a deep breath and paused before marching into her private chambers. "You heard?"

Leona Peterson closed the door of the reception area. "I heard."

Blythe hiked up her robes to reveal a pair of worn Nike running shoes and perched on the immaculate surface of her secretary's desk. "Drat the man! I should have thrown the book at him!"

"I thought you just did," Leona pointed out calmly as she tucked a strand of iron-gray hair back into the practical bun she had worn for the past thirty of her fifty-five years.

"Why did I let him get to me like that?" Blythe demanded, but then the temper went out of her eyes. "I actually cited him for contempt."

"Yes, you did, but it sounded to me like the 'Columbus Crusader' dug his own grave," Leona soothed as she handed Blythe the glass of iced tea she'd prepared as soon as the recess had been called. "Perhaps he didn't notice that the judge was a lady."

"In the courtroom, she isn't," Blythe retorted firmly.

Leona smiled at that, but was careful to hide her expression. The judge had been inordinately nervous about this case ever since it had appeared on the docket, but now wasn't the time to remind her of the purely feminine response she'd expressed upon seeing Patrick McBride's name. Leona, however, recalled every word of the heartfelt prayer Blythe had delivered to the heavens that day. "Lord, don't let me be swayed by a pair of laughing Irish eyes, a devil-may-care grin and a tall, sexy body. Give me the strength to do my job in the face of such overwhelming adversity and be ever mindful that justice is blind."

Blythe gave Leona a grateful look over the top of her glass as she downed the cold drink. Once her thirst was quenched, she admitted, "I'll have to give the man credit. With his reputation, I thought I'd be subjected to more than my fair share of Gaelic charm, but I saw not so much as a wee dram o' the stuff, did you?''

"So you threw the unchivalrous knave in the slammer,'' Leona suggested facetiously and waited for the inevitable rebuttal. When her judicial decisions came under fire, the youngest and only female member of the Franklin County Court of Domestic Relations could always be counted upon to quote the appropriate statutes, chapter and verse. Blythe Cramer never let her personal feelings interfere with the law.

"Lord, I hope that's not why I did it,'' was the unexpected response as Blythe hopped off the desk and walked slowly into her chambers.

"Your Honor?'' Leona hurried after her boss.

Blythe laughed at the older woman's stunned expression. "Close the door, Leona. I don't want anyone else to hear that the esteemed Judge Cramer might have made a less than impartial decision.'' She wiped a hand over her brow. "Good grief, you'd think with all the money that went into this new building, we'd be able to count on the air-conditioning to work.''

After stripping off her heavy robes, Blythe propped herself up on the window ledge to catch the summer breeze coming in through the only window that wasn't sealed. In a tank top and running shorts, her tanned skin gleaming with perspiration, she looked more like a young female athlete than a judge, but whatever her dress, Blythe's mind was never far away from the duties of her office. "The press will have a heyday if they get wind of this, and I've got enough to contend with as it is.''

Leona well understood what Blythe was saying. Blythe's appointment to the bench had aroused heated fire from all quarters, and every one of her decisions was subject to intense scrutiny. Since a member of the wealthy and staunchly Republican Cramer family could be found at almost every level of state government, Blythe's appointment by a partisan governor, who had strong political affiliations with the family, had screamed of nepotism. Although she had graduated at the top of her class at Harvard, was a highly qualified lawyer associated with one of the most prestigious firms in the state, had five years of experience clerking for her uncle, Judge Donald Cramer, Blythe still hadn't been considered qualified to complete his term of office.

While it was true that upon Donald Cramer's death, the family had pulled a few strings, called in their political favors to secure her appointment, such methods had been in force since the beginning of time. Blythe didn't approve of the system, but she was a realist and knew that the only way she'd ever have a chance for a judgeship was to wield some family clout. By doing so she had the same opportunity as anyone else to prove herself, and after serving the remaining two years of her uncle's term, she would have to seek election in her own right.

Until she could be voted in, however, her detractors would jump on her slightest indiscretion, trying to prove that a thirty-three-year-old woman was too young and inexperienced to hold such a responsible position. Leona fervently hoped that today's episode wouldn't be the catalyst they needed to prevent Blythe from securing office for another six years.

As soon as the door was closed, Leona stepped into her role as devil's advocate, a position she'd assumed early on in their relationship to forestall just such an occurrence.

Leona had gotten her first secretarial job in the courthouse when she'd been eighteen and now had over thirty-five years of experience behind her. She'd seen a score of judges come and go, and she knew when the state had been blessed with a good one. Blythe Cramer was good—very good—and Leona would do anything in her power to make sure the young woman stayed on the bench where she belonged.

"As I see it, Patrick McBride is as liberal as they come, and therefore a confrontation between him and you would be the perfect fodder for our political opponents to spread across the front pages. Word is, come next election, he's going to run for a seat in the House," Leona began, her voice tight with concern. "He's got the charm of a born politician and the looks to match. Women everywhere will clamor to give him their vote."

Blythe groaned. "Please don't tell me that just because he looks like the male lead in every woman's sexual fantasy, it can guarantee his election. I hope the liberation movement has gotten us beyond that point."

"That's just it," Leona advised sagely. "McBride is much more than a pretty face. He's worked to get where he is. He's perfect in the role of watchdog for the little guy. Having a successful family behind him hasn't hurt, either. His older brother, Sean, has earned the respect of conservatives and liberals alike."

"McBride and McBride." Blythe made a face. "All this town needed was a whole nest of those redheaded devils. Neal McBride is called 'Johnny Hustle,' and I've heard the youngest one, Kevin, is almost as flamboyant as Patrick. According to the gossip columns, women follow them around like sheep."

"So what did that prejudicial rich Republican spinster, Judge Cramer, do when faced with our handsome hero? How did she treat the man who was fighting to uphold the rights of the downtrodden?''

Blythe raised both hands and began pulling on her short black hair. "Ugh! That's disgusting! Do you honestly think anyone will see it that way?"

"Anyone with an ounce of political savvy will not only see it that way but run with it." Leona sat down in an overstuffed chair, crossed her arms over her ample bosom and inquired, "Now what were you saying about not making an impartial judgment?"

Her blue eyes wide with mock terror, Blythe formed her fingers into a cross and held them up between her and her tormentor. "Nothing! Not a thing. Those offending words never crossed my rich spinster lips."

"I should hope not." Leona nodded with approval. "So what do we do with the poor man who's been banished to the courthouse dungeon?"

Blythe jumped off the ledge and began pacing up and down the Oriental carpet. Her arms clasped behind her back, she recited, "We graciously accept his fine and apology in private, whereby our hero isn't publicly humiliated and will be less likely to bemoan his fate to the receptive ears of a liberal press. We uphold the fair nature of the court by hearing the remainder of the case without prejudice, and then we render an unbiased decision based on nothing but the facts."

Pausing for breath, she glanced at the clock, and a momentary panic darkened her eyes. "And we start now before some free-lance reporter gets curious about the unscheduled recess going on in courtroom four."

Leona gave the thumbs-up signal and retrieved Blythe's robe from the top of her desk. "It's already nine-thirty. I'll call maintenance again and see if they can't get the air-conditioning going. Otherwise you're going to swelter in this thing."

Blythe shrugged her shoulders as she replaced the heavy garment over her less-than-dignified-looking outfit. "No doubt about it. I'm on the hot seat today, and there's no relief in sight."

"For the flames of justice never stop burning."

Blythe gave a short laugh, then started walking toward the door. Before leaving the room, she stopped and looked over her shoulder. "Did I ever tell you that Patrick McBride and I attended the same elementary school?"

"No," Leona replied, taken aback.

"The same high school?"

"No."

"Graduated the same year from Harvard Law School and passed the bar on the same day?"

Leona paled. "Blythe? How well do you know this guy?"

"As well as anyone knows their nemesis, Leona," Blythe confirmed grimly, waited for Leona's astonished gasp, then marched out the door.

The holding unit had ten cells. Patrick McBride was the sole occupant of the last cell at the end of the long hall. He'd been spared the company of pimps in wide-brimmed hats, sleepy-eyed repeat offenders, drunkards, petty thieves and hardened criminals, all waiting to be sentenced. His sentence had already been handed down, and he'd been left alone to contemplate the error of his ways.

Mitch Dobs, the bailiff for Judge Cramer's court, had managed to keep a straight face until he'd escorted his "prisoner" into the elevator, but the ex-marine had started to grin as soon as they'd begun their descent to the basement. "Looks like you tweaked the wrong tail this time, McBride. That'll teach ya."

It had taken all of Patrick's fortitude not to make the crude comeback that remark had brought to mind. No, any thoughts he had about the lovely Judge Cramer's even lovelier behind were better left unsaid. Neither had he mentioned all the things he'd like to teach the woman that had absolutely nothing to do with the law.

Unfortunately, ever since he'd been locked up, those things were all he'd been able to think about. How he'd like to tutor the woman who, beyond the courthouse walls, was often referred to as the "Iron Maiden," in the fine art of lovemaking, teach her to let loose and enjoy all that passion he saw hiding behind the lush, long lashes of her incredible navy-blue eyes.

He wanted to kiss the slight pout in her delectable lower lip, caress the silken skin that was magnolia white in the winter and creamy peach in the summer. Yes, Blythe Cramer was a delicate blossom that with the right tender loving care could bloom into a magnificent flower, an all-American beauty rose.

"And you're a bloomin' idiot, McBride, if you think you'll ever be caretaker in that exclusive garden," Patrick berated himself under his breath. After this little episode, he'd be firmly entrenched in her mind as the lowlife grub that had been worming holes in her peace of mind since the first grade.

"Hell!" he cursed loudly, tossed his suit coat on the narrow bottom bunk, which was suspended on heavy chains from the back wall, then threw himself down on the plastic mattress.

"Is that your comment on the weather conditions down here, counselor, or an indication of your present state of mind?"

At the sound of Blythe's voice, Patrick sat up so fast that he misjudged his distance and hit his forehead on the steel springs of the upper bunk. A shaft of pain lanced between his eyes, and he couldn't prevent a succinct expletive from reaching a prim set of judicial ears.

Patrick pressed his palms over the painful area and groaned, "For mouthing obscenities, I throw myself on the mercy of the court."

As the first trickle of blood seeped through his fingers, down his wrists and stained the crisp white cuffs of his shirt, he concluded, "That done, I now intend to quietly bleed to death."

"Open this door, deputy, then go find some bandages," Blythe ordered, and as soon as the door swung open, she went over to Patrick.

"You'd better lie back." Sinking to her knees, Blythe placed her hands on Patrick's shoulders and pushed him down on the bare mattress. She grabbed his suit coat and plucked the neatly folded lawn handkerchief out of the hand-stitched breast pocket.

Brushing his bloodied hands aside, she pressed the expensive material down on the gash in his forehead. "I can see the papers now. 'Governor Wainright's Judicial Appointee Sentences Valiant Public Defender to Jail, Where He Suffers Near-Fatal Head Wound.'"

Patrick would have laughed, but Blythe's tone was serious. Besides, he'd waited almost eighteen years to feel her hands on him again, and he was going to enjoy it while it lasted. God knows how long it would be before he'd have the pleasure repeated. Thirty seconds later he'd made up his mind that if he had anything to do with it, it wouldn't be very long at all.

"Scoot over so I can apply more pressure. We've got to stop the bleeding," Blythe requested, unaware that her patient wasn't the least bit concerned with the possibility that he'd sustained a serious wound.

"Okay." Patrick was more than happy to oblige. Sharing any kind of bed with her, under any kind of circumstance, was a dream come true. He groaned, closing his eyes as the rounded curve of her thigh pressed against his hip, and a soft, full breast brushed against his shirtfront. She smelled like flowers—fragrant roses. Heaven help him, she still smelled like roses!

"You're not the type who faints at the sight of his own blood, are you?" Blythe asked nervously, using her free hand to stroke away the stubborn thatch of dark auburn hair that she remembered always had a tendency to fall over his forehead. His skin was far whiter than normal. "Patrick? Patrick, are you all right?"

"Uh-huh," Patrick managed weakly from the depths of an euphoric daze. She'd not only called him by his first name, sounding genuinely concerned, but was running her long elegant fingers through his hair.

"Here you go, Your Honor." The deputy was back with a first-aid kit and a handful of damp paper towels. "Douse that cut with some antiseptic, and he'll live to fight another day."

The highly amused tone of the city jailer roused Patrick from his dreamy state, but it was still an unpleasant shock when smooth linen was replaced by rough paper. "Ouch," he protested, but in a voice strong enough to dispel any further doubts concerning his light-headed condition. He tried to sit up, but Blythe prevented him.

"Stay put until we get you cleaned up and bandaged," she ordered briskly, then proceeded to do just that.

Ten minutes later Patrick was on his feet. He glanced down at his blood-splattered shirt. "I can't go back into court like this."

"True," Blythe declared consideringly, then made a decision. She turned to the deputy. "George, we're taking Mr. McBride to my chambers. We need to get there without anyone seeing us. Is that possible?"

"Follow me," George Riley said. Across the hall was a door that led down another flight of stairs to a sub-basement. Moments later they were inside a freight elevator and heading for the seventh floor.

George acted as lookout, but since the other three courts were in session, the back hall off the judicial chambers was empty. Within seconds Patrick and Blythe were safely inside her two-room office. Leona was sitting behind her desk but stood up the instant she saw who was accompanying her boss.

"Merciful heavens!" she exclaimed in horror. "What happened? You didn't bust him over the head, did you?"

Patrick lifted an inquiring brow, his green eyes dancing with mischief. "Have a tendency toward violence, do you, Your Honor?"

Blythe didn't find the question funny and neither did her secretary. The two women exchanged looks, and Patrick was taken aback by their expression. They appeared to be frightened, but of what? Surely not him?

What did they think he was going to do? Sue? On what grounds, he wondered. As far as he was concerned, the damage to his head was his own damned fault. He'd be just as happy if no one else ever found out about it.

"Patrick McBride, Leona Peterson," Blythe announced as she shut the office door.

Patrick nodded at the woman who was looking at him as if he were a snake who'd just crawled out from underneath a rock. Again he was struck by the feeling that the two women were aware of something that he didn't know about, but should. "Hey! This isn't such a tragedy. I sat up too fast and hit my head. No big deal. Accidents like that happen every day."

"Not in my court, they don't," Blythe stated shortly.

"Oh, I forgot." Patrick grinned. "Not a single blemish would dare to mar Judge Cramer's sterling reputation."

Both women glared at him as Blythe said, "I suggest we send Leona out for a clean suit for you, counselor. Where should she go, to your home or your office?"

"That's not necessary. I'll go downstairs and call a cab. I can be back in less than a half hour."

"No!" Blythe and Leona shouted in unison.

Patrick's expression became quizzical as he tried to figure out what he'd said to bring about such a strong reaction. He felt a spurt of temper when Blythe hastily pointed out that he still hadn't fulfilled the requirements the court had set down to erase the contempt charge against him.

"You and I can see to the matter, Mr. McBride, while Leona goes for a fresh set of clothes."

"Must you stick this close to the letter of the law, Your Honor?" Patrick asked cuttingly. "In this case, a little leniency can't hurt either one of us, and I'm sure your secretary has better things to do than run errands for me. When I get back, I'll be more than happy to apologize for my earlier remarks in court, pay my fine and get on with the proceedings."

"Sticking close to the letter of the law is my job, Mr. McBride," Blythe retorted, struggling to contain her own temper. She knew very well that Patrick would like nothing better than to parade through the halls of justice in his bloodied condition, but she wasn't going to let him get away with it.

"Fine," Patrick snapped, aware that she wasn't going to change her mind. "Mrs. Peterson, if you wouldn't mind, I'd like to send along a note for you to give to my brother Sean."

"What kind of note?" Blythe asked suspiciously.

Patrick's green eyes narrowed with annoyance as he bit out, "A note that tells him where to look for my underwear."

"Your underwear didn't sustain any damage," Blythe countered, then heard Leona's strangled attempt to swallow a laugh. She immediately felt like a fool for being so mistrustful that she wouldn't even give the man the benefit of the doubt concerning the condition of his shorts.

"Shall I produce the physical evidence necessary to prove otherwise?" Patrick challenged, reaching for his belt buckle.

A lengthy silence followed wherein Blythe tried and failed to control the wild flush that crept up her neck and into her cheeks. She knew damned well that Patrick intended to send some sort of message to his brother that would cause trouble for her, but she wasn't quite prepared to watch him strip down to his shorts in order to prove he was lying. "Get him a piece of paper and a pen, Leona."

"Certainly, Your Honor."

Patrick's lips twitched with suppressed laughter as he accepted the writing supplies and bent over Leona's desk. He didn't know what Blythe was afraid he might say to his brother, but if she saw what he actually did write down, it would provide more fuel for that beautiful pink blush she was wearing.

Sean,
Give this woman a complete set of my clothes. The gorgeous Judge Cramer has commandeered all of mine. Don't tell a soul about this until I explain, but this has been my lucky day.

Patrick

"Do you have an envelope I might use, Mrs. Peterson?" Patrick requested politely.

"Why didn't you just write it in secret code?" Blythe muttered in disgust.

"It wasn't necessary." Patrick slipped the paper into the envelope Leona gave him and made a great show of licking the flap. After assuring himself it was firmly sealed, he handed the envelope to Leona. "Unlike some people I know, I have very little to hide."

"And what's that supposed to mean?"

Leona heard Blythe's heated question as she quietly left the room. She smiled. For some reason, she no longer believed her boss had anything to fear from Patrick McBride. Oh, it was obvious that a momentous explosion would one day erupt between them, but she didn't think it would have any effect on future elections. Increase the population maybe, but not alter the popular vote.

TWO

My, my, but you're touchy," Patrick drawled as he surveyed the interior of the office. "But then you always were."

Blythe couldn't believe her ears. In the twenty-seven years that she'd been aware of Patrick McBride's existence, the two of them had spoken only a few times. All through their early school days, they'd only been assigned to the same classroom once, and they had traveled in widely different circles of friends. At Harvard they'd taken the same subjects, but luckily they'd been on different schedules and had rarely run into each other.

Other than the fact that she'd shared the limelight with him on countless occasions, what little else she knew about him had been learned from other people, and any information he had about her had to have been gathered in the same way. "That's an interesting observation to make. On what do you base your judgment, counselor?''

Patrick gazed into her eyes, glad to see that the fear he'd seen in them a few minutes earlier was no longer present. Even so, one day soon, he was going to find out what had brought about that strange reaction. For the time being, however, he was content to talk of other things. ''For so many years I'd look over my shoulder, and there you were, right behind me.''

''Right beside you, and that's no proof that I'm touchy.''

''Blythe Cramer,'' Patrick said, ignoring her comment and repeating her name as if it were a dirty word. ''In any award I've ever won, any test I've taken or contest I've entered, that name has always shared the same line with mine. In most cases, since alphabetical order was the rule, your name came first. I didn't like it, but no matter how hard I tried I'd see or hear—for academic excellence in this subject or that—Blythe Cramer and Patrick McBride.''

Blythe bit her lip to keep from laughing. How often had she been plagued by the same feelings? Just once she'd have liked to have had sole possession of the gold star, the blue ribbon, be the only name at the top of the list. Because of him, it had never happened.

They'd even passed the state bar exam with the same score, a piece of information she'd pried out of a friend who'd clerked in the application office. She'd made a point of not telling anyone her own score, but wondered if Patrick had somehow found out what it was. She hoped he hadn't, and had spent the past seven years worrying about it.

''I understand how you feel, McBride,'' she allowed. ''But that still doesn't tell me how you reached the erroneous conclusion I was touchy. It sounds as if you were the touchy one, not me. So what if some people assumed that my name appeared first because I was just the teensiest bit better than you? You and I know the truth."

"Is this off the record?" Patrick called over his shoulder as he walked into the inner office and took the chair in front of Blythe's desk. He rested his head on the cushioned back, dangled his arms off the sides and stretched out his long legs on the floor. "Mmmm, very comfy."

"Make yourself right at home," Blythe advised scathingly as she hurried after him and took up her position behind the desk. "You were saying?"

Blythe realized she was showing an inordinate amount of interest in his personal judgment of her, but her curiosity was stronger than her pride. Maybe someday she'd have the opportunity to reveal a few assessments she'd made concerning his character, but in the meantime she was hoping to hear his about her, even if the smile on his face was disgustingly smug.

"Off the record?" he insisted.

"Certainly."

"Take this morning, for example," Patrick began, the sparkle in his eyes giving evidence of how much he was enjoying himself. "Most judges would have overlooked my comments, accepted that a certain amount of judge baiting is the stock and trade of any good defense lawyer. However, because you're overly concerned with maintaining your precious dignity, you're much too sensitive."

"Hogwash," Blythe scoffed, disappointed in him for presenting such a flimsy case. "You'll have to do better than that."

"All right," Patrick agreed. "Let's go back to yesteryear. Remember our sophomore year, the Fire and Ice Dance? I was king and you were queen?"

Blythe gulped. That was a memory she'd repressed so deeply that it hadn't bothered her in years. She had hoped and prayed that Patrick, too, had long since forgotten it, but here he was dredging it up with obvious relish.

That fateful night, she'd eventually given in to her mother's pleading and worn a flaming red dress. The low neckline had highlighted the embarrassing rate of development she'd undergone that year, and the spaghetti straps had barely been up to the strain. Although she and Patrick had arrived and left with their own dates, the king and queen had been expected to launch the evening's festivities. After walking arm in arm down a long red carpet, they had been seated side by side in armchairs decorated as royal thrones. Then, though neither of them had liked the idea, they had been required to dance the first dance together.

"I can see that you do remember," Patrick said, his eyes centered on the twin spots of color burning in her cheeks.

Blythe's lips tightened. "I was fifteen. I admit that adolescent girls are touchy about…about certain things, but I hope I've gained a little more sophistication since then."

"Let's find out." Patrick flashed her the same audacious grin he'd had that long ago night when he'd deliberately pulled her against him and held her much too closely. "Care to dance?"

"Don't be ridiculous." She caught his eyes probing the heavy material of her robes, and she wanted to kick him. He was outrageous! Always had been, always would be.

"Then I can't prove my case." Patrick waggled an accusing finger at her. "Wouldn't you say that's obstructing justice, Your Honor?"

"Off the record?"

"By all means," Patrick allowed magnanimously.

"I'd say you were an impossible, conceited boy who's developed into an even more impossible and conceited man. One of these days, McBride, some woman is going to give you your comeuppance, and I'd give anything to see it."

"Since we're not speaking lawyer to judge but man to woman, I'd like to say that I'd give anything to see your breasts again. When your strap broke last time, I only got a partial view."

He paused as if savoring a favorite memory, but in actuality he was savoring the utterly appalled look on her face. "After all these years," he continued, "I'll bet you're even more beautifully mature." His green eyes glued to Blythe's face, he relaxed back in the chair and waited for her to demonstrate just how touchy she still was.

Halfway through his speech, Blythe's mouth had dropped open in disbelief. She was too irate to enjoy the tingle that passed through her and proclaimed her a very passionate woman. Patrick McBride was more than outrageous, he was a scheming, ruthless devil. Blythe's stunned brain kicked back into gear as she silently acknowledged the bait he'd just used to cleverly lure her into his trap.

"Yes, I am," she conceded in what she hoped was an even tone. "I've also matured emotionally. You, on the other hand, still operate in the same manner you did in your teens.''

Patrick's deep chuckle was as attractive as it was irritating. She had proven that she was equal to anything he cared to dish out, and all she'd gotten for the effort was that low, husky rumble of male amusement. She couldn't wait to see the last of him. To that end, she opened a desk drawer and took out a voucher.

While filling in the appropriate spaces, she said, ''Let's get back to the business at hand, counselor, and this is definitely judge to lawyer.'' She pushed the paper across the desk and held out a pen. ''The fine was fifty dollars.''

Patrick lifted his suit coat off his lap and riffled the pockets for his checkbook. Taking the pen she offered, he wrote out a check and signed his name below hers on the voucher. ''Paid in full, Your Honor.'' He handed his check back to her.

''Thank you.'' Trying to emulate Patrick's nonchalant manner, Blythe leaned back in her chair, rested her head on the leather cushion and stretched her legs out as far as they would reach. ''I believe your apology is the next order of business.''

''Nice shoes, Your Honor,'' Patrick complimented, grinning down at the bare ankles and dirty canvas toes peeping out at him from beneath her desk.

Blythe sat up straight but didn't give him the satisfaction of verbally proving that at least one of his charges was true. She wasn't so concerned with protecting her dignity that she couldn't take a little teasing. ''Thank you,'' she returned easily and even managed to smile. ''They're comfortable.''

Since he was sweating in his shirt sleeves, and she didn't appear to be suffering to a far greater degree, he would have bet his last dollar she was wearing next to nothing beneath her robes. "If you want to make yourself even more comfortable, feel free to take off that hot robe. It's like a furnace in here."

Patrick's conciliatory suggestion was anything but and Blythe knew it. "I'm fine, thank you."

"You look miserable, Your Honor," Patrick disagreed, but was careful to keep a polite distance in his tone. "Even without the uniform, I'm not likely to forget that you're a judge."

And a beautiful woman, he thought. Sexy as anything, but still a judge.

"Your concern is appreciated, Mr. McBride, but I'd appreciate your apology even more." Blythe was determined to stay in control of a situation Patrick was equally determined would get out of hand. "Contempt for the court is a serious transgression. I hope in the future you will treat it as such and not use your baiting tactics to such an unwise extent again."

Patrick captured her elusive gaze with an intense look, and no matter how hard she tried, Blythe couldn't glance away. His soft-spoken voice felt like an intimate caress, and she shivered with each word he uttered. "I'm sincerely sorry, Your Honor, for disobeying your orders, insulting the court and attempting to influence your judgment. I promise not to do so again."

"Apology accepted, Mr. McBride," Blythe declared in a small voice. She cleared the sudden thickness in her throat, then spoke more briskly, "I'll inform the clerk that court can resume in a half hour. Leona should be back by then."

They stood up together, Blythe for the purpose of vacating the room and Patrick to acknowledge the leave-taking of a lady. His courtly gesture disarmed her, and Blythe accepted it with an awkward nod. "My office is at your disposal until eleven, Mr. McBride."

Blythe sipped a soda and watched the clock. It was almost eleven. Was Patrick finished with her office, or was he still getting dressed? From the empty office across the hall, she'd witnessed Leona's arrival with his clean clothes, but that had been over twenty minutes ago, and he still hadn't vacated her private chambers. What on earth was he doing in there?

An image of him prancing around her office in his birthday suit was disconcerting, to say the least. What was even more upsetting was that whenever she forced that mental picture out of her mind another haunted her, and it was one she hadn't conjured up out of her imagination. That dance, that humiliating dance they'd had together in the tenth grade.

"Let's get this over with," Patrick had urged rudely, grabbing her hand and practically dragging her out onto the dance floor.

Worried about the revealing design of her flimsy dress, she was self-conscious enough that night without his hauling her against his chest and keeping her there by clamping an arm around her waist. Feeling stiff and awkward, she heard the snickers of his football teammates and the giggles of her fellow cheerleaders as he whirled her around and around the dance floor. With her black hair and red dress, his auburn hair and black tux, they made a striking couple, but one of his buddies felt her looks surpassed his. "Too bad, McBride! You've got the same stats on paper, but Cramer stacks up better in the clinches."

"Oh!" Blythe gasped furiously.

"Ignore him. He's just jealous." Patrick went into a series of quick steps and turns that left her breathless and clinging.

"Stop holding me so close," she pleaded desperately once she was capable, but Patrick was enjoying himself too much to acquiesce.

She knew he was trying to get back at her for all the times he'd tried to best her and failed. "I've had enough of this."

"Loosen up, Cramer," Patrick muttered in her ear. "Or people will know there's something I can do better than you. You're dancing like a robot."

To Blythe's everlasting thanks, other couples came out to join them, and they were no longer the subject of everyone's attention and comments. As additional dancers crowded on to the floor, Blythe felt one of her straps let go. Her bodice started slipping, and she instinctively pressed herself closer to Patrick to keep it from falling all the way down. She'd never forgiven him for what he did next.

Grabbing her hands, he pulled her arms around his waist and kept them in that position by shackling her wrists in one of his hands. His other hand was free to come up beneath her long black hair and encircle her nape. Pushing her head down on his shoulder, he made it appear as if she were enjoying their intimate embrace.

She struggled briefly, but ceased at once as the silky fabric of her dress slipped down farther, exposing a rosy nipple. Blythe's heart was pounding frantically. She was terrified that any second someone might notice. Patrick did. Blythe knew he wasn't being chivalrous when he ensured that disclosure would be reserved for the two of them.

Keeping hold of her wrists, he swept her waist-length hair over her right shoulder, concealing her semi-nakedness behind a silky black curtain. "You've filled out very nicely, Cramer. I'm impressed."

His green eyes laughed down at her as she lifted her head to tell him just how much she hated him. "Be good," he warned. "You know what will happen if I back off."

Blythe reddened, and Patrick had the nerve to suggest that she'd better stick to him like glue until their dance was over. Since there was no way she could do otherwise without humiliating herself even further, she complied.

"You're a detestable, low-down snake, Patrick McBride," she whispered fiercely into the side of his neck. "I despise everything about you."

"I felt the same way about you until tonight," Patrick returned softly. His voice sounded strangled, his tone thick. "Now I know there are some things about you I like very much."

Blythe was painfully aware of what "things" he was referring to, and she couldn't stand it a second longer. Tears of embarrassment welled up in her eyes. She hid her face in his shirt and tried to blink them away, but with no success. She followed his movements blindly, too miserable to care about anything but the moment when her suffering would come to an end.

That moment came more quickly than she'd expected. The band was still playing, but Patrick had stopped dancing. She forced herself to open her eyes and saw that he had guided her across the floor to the door of the girls' locker room.

Keeping himself between her and anyone who might be watching them, Patrick pulled up her broken strap until her breast was decently covered. Blythe's fingers quickly took the place of his on her bodice. Her head down, she couldn't look at him, would never be able to look at him again.

"Please don't cry, Blythe," he begged. "You're too beautiful to cry. I'm really sorry."

Go away! Blythe entreated silently, but he didn't move, and she couldn't escape into the locker room until he did.

"No one but me noticed anything, and I promise I'll never tell another living soul."

Blythe nodded. She couldn't find the courage to lift her head and face him, even though she realized that was what he was waiting for and that he wouldn't leave her alone until she did.

Patrick completed the impossible task for her. Gently, he cupped her chin and forced her to look at him. He gazed into her tear-drenched eyes, and the sight seemed to cause him pain. A muscle jerked in his cheek as he vowed quietly, "I never meant to... Jeez, I'm sorry."

Speechlessly Blythe stared up at him. In the next second Patrick's contrite expression changed to something else, something far more shocking. Blythe saw his jaw go tight and his lips soften just before he lowered them to hers. The kiss was no more than the light touch of a feather, over quickly, but it inspired an emotion in Blythe she had never felt in her entire life. Sheer heart-stopping panic.

Without saying another word, Patrick turned on his heel and walked away. Blythe fled into the locker room. By the time she'd composed herself enough to come out, Patrick and his date had left the dance. Blythe's date was requested to take her home very shortly thereafter.

Once she'd been home in her room, she'd made a solemn promise to herself that had helped her get through the next few days. She was going to do all in her power to ensure that Patrick McBride never bested her in anything again. Until today, that promise had never been broken.

Down the hall from the empty office where Blythe was reliving the past, Patrick was contemplating the future. He'd finished changing and doubted anyone would notice the small bandage on his forehead. Since he didn't want to add to his embarrassment by explaining how he'd gotten hurt, he'd combed his hair forward, making it barely visible.

That done, he had propped his feet up on Blythe's desk and was currently staring at the framed picture of her that hung on the wall. Judge Blythe Cramer. The photo didn't do her justice. Thank God he was no longer going to be intimidated by that frigid little smile and imperious stare that had put him off for so many years. If he'd known in his school days what he knew now, the woman would have had him to contend with far sooner than this.

He couldn't wait to finish the Wynbush case so Blythe couldn't use the potential conflict of interest as an excuse not to see him. He stole another glance at the wall clock. Five more minutes and he'd have to leave her private domain, relinquish his enjoyment of her flowery scent, which lingered in the room and was more intoxicating to him than champagne.

He ran his fingers over the polished mahogany of her desk. His eyes lit up as an idea hit him. He reached for the pen in her desk stand, then found a piece of blank paper in the top drawer.

His note thanked her for the use of her office and ended, depending upon one's perspective, with the warning or the assurance that he planned to see her again soon. He signed the note with a flourish, then centered it on her desk blotter. A personal reminder of him would be the first thing Blythe would find when she returned to her desk after trying his case. He intended to make certain she'd stop relegating him to the back of her mind.

"Mr. McBride?" Leona knocked on the closed door, opened it, then announced, "Judge Cramer is going down the back hall to the courtroom. It won't help your case if you're late."

"I'm on my way, Mrs. Peterson." Patrick bestowed a beatific smile on the woman as he sauntered past her on his way out the door. With a thick Irish brogue, he asked, "Now isn't it a grand day we're havin', colleen?"

"If you say so, Mr. McBride," Leona replied dryly, but smiled back, having no more resistance to Patrick's potent male charm than any other member of her sex. "Take my advice, and don't try your luck in there."

Patrick turned back to throw her a jaunty salute and quipped, "My dear woman, boys try their luck; men risk it."

"One moment, please, counselor." Blythe had interrupted Patrick's interrogation of the witness to ask her own question. "Miss Baker, are you saying that the foster mother is paid close to six hundred dollars per month to look after the Wynbush children, and welfare was paying the natural mother a little over three hundred for the same thing?"

"Yes," Madelaine Baker admitted but was quick to add, "She was supposed to work part-time—"

"Your Honor, that's the point I've been trying to make," Patrick cut in, but Blythe gestured him to silence. Sensing she was about to do the rest of his work for him, Patrick shrugged and walked back to the defense table. He gave his frightened client a reassuring wink, crossed his arms over his chest and waited for Blythe to reach the same conclusions he'd had when reviewing the case.

"Miss Wynbush was told she had to work part-time?" Blythe resumed her questioning.

"Yes," Madelaine answered.

"Does the foster mother work?"

"She can't. That's forbidden under state law."

"I see," Blythe concluded, and didn't like what she saw. "The witness may step down."

Madelaine Baker hurried to comply with the terse order and was back in her seat by the time Blythe said, "Will counsel approach the bench."

Patrick arrived a few steps before Lloyd Hastings, who was representing the state. He realized his presence wasn't needed in the upcoming audience, but he didn't want to miss the fireworks. He was supremely grateful that this time someone else would be taking the brunt of Blythe's judicial anger.

"Mr. Hastings," Blythe began. "Were you aware that the Department of Social Welfare is willing to pay a stranger almost twice as much to take care of these children as their natural mother?"

"Well, Your Honor—"

"What kind of system is that?"

Hastings struggled to find a suitable answer, but Blythe didn't wait for one. "Never mind! I don't want to hear it."

A few moments later, Sheena Wynbush was awarded custody of her children with the provision that they were to stay in the foster home until such time as Sheena, in the opinion of her social worker, was emotionally and financially able to provide for them on her own. After delivering a stern closing statement that advised the state to keep a closer watch on the inequities that women and children must deal with, Judge Cramer dismissed the court.

"If McBride wanted to make me feel like a louse for citing him with contempt, he certainly did a good job," Blythe complained to Leona as she disrobed in her office. "No wonder he was all over that Baker woman."

"Two wrongs don't make a right," Leona reminded her, but she could tell that her words fell on deaf ears.

"Thank God that poor woman hired a good attorney and came away believing that justice serves not only the rich but the poor."

Leona nodded. "Both you and McBride can be proud of yourselves today."

"Well, he can sleep tonight with a clear conscience," Blythe verified broodingly. "If he doesn't have a blinding headache from that knock he took on the head."

"You aren't responsible for that. He did that to himself."

"Right," Blythe said, but without much conviction. "Can you have a few sandwiches brought in, Leona? I want to go over the rest of this afternoon's cases before the lunch recess is over."

Distracted by her guilty conscience, Blythe didn't notice that the air-conditioning was working again until she was a few feet away from her desk. "What a relief! I thought we'd suffer in this heat all week."

"You're going to catch cold if you stay in those shorts," Leona warned. "Why don't you change clothes."

"Good idea," Blythe agreed, but not out of any concern for her health. She was positive that some time today she was in for another confrontation with Patrick McBride, and this time she was going to be better prepared. Too bad her closet didn't contain a suit of steel armor.

Retracing her steps, Blythe told Leona to inform any visitors that she'd gone out for lunch, then closed the door. Coward, she scolded herself as she stripped off her shorts and top. She was standing before the closet in bra and panties, considering her choices, when the phone rang. Evidently Leona was screening her guests but not her calls.

Blythe pulled a pink shirtwaist dress down from its hanger, then hurried across the room to answer the phone. Holding the dress over one arm, she sat down on her desk and scooted in a few inches in order to reach the receiver. Before it was halfway to her ear, her eyes lit on the note Patrick had left behind for her to find. His bold signature fairly leaped off the paper.

Blythe jumped off the desk and the phone went with her. The receiver flew out of her hand as the phone landed with a bang and skidded across the polished hardwood floor. Blythe winced when the receiver bounced twice, then flipped over.

Kneeling down, she snatched it up, sounding slightly out of breath as she spoke into it. "I'm so sorry. I dropped the phone."

No response.

"Eh . . . this is Judge Cramer. To whom am I speaking?"

"If I didn't know better, Your Honor, I'd think you knew exactly to whom you were speaking."

It was Blythe's turn for silence, but evidently Patrick didn't expect any response. "I feel like celebrating, Blythe," he drawled seductively into her ear. "If I asked very sweetly, would you consider joining me for dinner this evening?"

Three

***

Don't you think it slightly inappropriate to invite the judge who heard the case to a victory celebration?" Blythe managed to convey a reserve she was far from feeling. "A lawyer may win or lose, Mr. McBride, but the judge must remain impartial. That's not to say I'm not happy for Ms. Wynbush."

"I'm not celebrating the conclusion of the Wynbush case, Blythe," Patrick put in smoothly, refusing to let her stuffy little speech douse his good spirits. "I want to celebrate our getting back together again after all these years."

"Getting back together!" Blythe choked out. At the sound of his amused chuckle, she managed to bite back further comment. He was baiting her again, and she'd already chomped down hard on the lure. However, she had no intention of running with the line. "I'm sorry, McBride, but I don't find that cause for celebration."

"Well, at least you're sorry about it." Patrick could almost picture her open mouth as he concluded, "But not half as sorry as I am. It appears I have my work cut out for me."

"I don't have any idea what you're talking about."

A soft sigh preceded his next words. "I'd like to show you I'm not the same guy you knew back in high school, Blythe. If you give me a chance, I think you'll find we've got a lot in common."

Without thinking, Blythe retorted, "What will that prove? I already know we've got a lot in common." She almost dropped the phone when she heard his laugh, that sexy, blarney-coated laugh that had drawn her instant attention from the very first time she'd heard it. It had lost none of its effectiveness. "Are you asking me out on a date, McBride?"

"I'm asking you out to dinner," he returned easily.

Blythe wanted further clarification and didn't care if she sounded old-fashioned and foolish as she pressed, "For reasons that have nothing to do with our respective professions?"

"To eat, drink and be merry," he verified.

Blythe hadn't known exactly what to expect from him and still wasn't certain if he was being wholly truthful with her. What if over an appeasing dinner and drinks, he showed her a press release of his recent and highly inopportune visit to the holding tank? What if he'd turned vindictive over the years, and at her expense, planned to use the incident to promote his image as a political activist? Or worse, what if he wanted to use it to gain something even more personal? He was well aware that she couldn't afford any bad press.

She had seen desire in his eyes more than once today. Patrick had earned a reputation as a womanizer. Maybe she was the next one on his list. If he had no scruples, he wouldn't care how he got her into his bed, just as long as he did. He could promise to keep quiet in exchange for...

"I'm not asking you to make a life-and-death decision here, Blythe," Patrick interrupted her thoughts. His tone was slightly irritated. "All we're talking about is dinner and a little socializing."

"Are we?" Blythe countered, unaware of the quaver in her voice that revealed the extent of her worry. As soon as she'd asked the question, she realized she was probably being ridiculous. He'd made a simple request and deserved an answer. Besides, no matter what her reservations, she wanted to go. It had been so long since she'd gone out with an exciting, attractive man. "Dinner sounds nice. What time and where?"

"I thought I'd make reservations at André's for around seven-thirty. Do you like French food?" Patrick asked.

Blythe sensed his relief when she answered in the affirmative. He probably thought she'd give him just as hard a time over his choice of restaurant as she had his invitation to dinner.

Not giving her the chance to change her mind, Patrick quickly went on, "Great. Give me your address, and I'll pick you up about seven. We can have a drink in the lounge beforehand."

"André's is close enough to the courthouse that I can walk over. I have to hear two more cases this afternoon and have quite a bit of other work to catch up on before tomorrow, so how about if I meet you over there?"

"If you like," Patrick agreed, but it sounded as if he'd have rather picked her up. "Afterward I'll drive you home."

"No need," Blythe replied. "I've got my car with me today."

"What the hell kind of a date is that?" Patrick blustered. "We get together for dinner, and that's it?"

"All you mentioned was dinner," Blythe reminded him, unable to keep the laughter out of her voice. It was fun to tease him just to see how he'd react and exciting to be kept constantly on her toes. "It's not my normal practice to date fellow members of the bar."

"Don't worry," Patrick assured her silkily before he hung up, "I'll give you all the practice you'll ever need. See you tonight."

It took Blythe several seconds to replace her own receiver while she digested his parting shot. Exciting or not, she wondered if she'd just made a very big mistake. The young Patrick McBride had always aroused a strong reaction in her, but today she'd discovered his appeal had grown even more intense over the years and her resistance pathetically weak. The adult Patrick was one hundred proof male and could intoxicate a woman with a look.

The sound of his voice made her go soft as a marshmallow, and his laughter toasted her insides. How was she ever going to hold her own with him for the length of time it took to eat an entire dinner? A multicourse meal, if André's hadn't recently changed menus. That question went unanswered as Blythe returned to work.

In court an hour later, Blythe had trouble concentrating on the case, *Lansing* v. *Lansing*. Deciding on an adequate divorce settlement for a woman who had enough wealth in her own right to buy half the state seemed a waste of court time and taxpayers' money. In fact, it was difficult to conjure up much sympathy for either party. Both attorneys had reputations for representing only the wealthiest clients, and Blythe knew their outrageous fees would be a mere drop in the bucket when compared to the couple's mutual assets. Their corporate interests alone looked like a page out of Dunn & Bradstreet.

Patrick McBride wouldn't have represented either one of them. He wasn't in law for the money. One more thing the two of them had in common. That thought did nothing to ease Blythe's anxiety about getting involved with him.

Though her mind continued to stray, Blythe willed herself to pay proper attention as counsel listed Valerie Lansing's current debts and monthly needs. She even managed to appear attentive as the woman's lawyer submitted a plea concerning her present state of extreme mental duress that required the services of a notoriously expensive psychiatrist. In the end, after hearing heated debate from both sides, Blythe gratefully accepted the compromise solution put forth by the soon-to-be ex-husband's lawyer.

Among other things, it gave Mrs. Lansing a huge block of blue chip stock, the income from three apartments in Florida, sole ownership of the beach property in Hawaii and the ancestral home in Ohio. Besides an equally lucrative stock portfolio, the husband was left with the family farm in Kentucky and a string of racehorses, a villa in the south of France and a penthouse in Manhattan. As far as Blythe was concerned, neither party would endure financial hardship due to the divorce, even if the wife appeared to have suffered such an inconsolable loss that she needed her young handsome attorney's assistance in order to leave the courtroom.

Blythe was happy she didn't have to witness more than a few seconds of the woman's dramatic exit. She left the bench immediately upon dismissing the court. "Any calls?" she asked Leona on the way into her chambers, half hoping Patrick had had second thoughts and called to cancel their dinner. If she was this nervous already, what would she be like by seven?

"Just one," Leona said, and was surprised by Blythe's stricken expression. "No need to look like that. It was only your mother, checking to see if you're going out to the house for that charity luncheon she's hosting Sunday afternoon. Who'd you think it was?"

"Mother," Blythe lied, a nonsensical smile on her face as she passed Leona's desk, heading for her office. "Call her back and tell her I wouldn't miss it."

"But you hate those things."

"Not today," Blythe replied mysteriously, then shook her head as if to clear it. "Today it looks like I'm in charity with the world. Ask me anything, Leona. I'll probably do it."

"How about giving me a raise?"

Already inside her office, Blythe poked her head back around the door. "Leona, would you really pit this poor lamb against that administrative lion, Judge Abernathy? Your new computer typewriter has already put me over budget."

"Forget I asked." Leona got up to fetch Blythe a fresh glass of iced tea. "Ever since I left his office and asked to be reassigned to you, that old skinflint's just been looking for a chance to wipe me off his books."

"Not while I'm around," Blythe guaranteed, then walked over to her desk to read Patrick's note one more time before she had to reappear in court for the next case.

* * *

Patrick parked his car in the alley behind the Stag's Head and entered the off-campus pub through the rear door. Dropping in on their parents' place before going separate ways for the evening was almost a daily ritual for the McBride brothers, and one that was usually enjoyable. Today, however, since he'd missed his brothers at the office, Patrick had a good idea what was waiting for him inside—the Irish inquisition. At least it was still early enough that there would be few customers to eavesdrop on the festivities.

"Who's up front?" he asked Nolan Rooney, long-time family friend and cook who was standing behind the grill flipping hamburgers.

"You're the last of them, boyo." Nolan waved a beefy arm toward the wide swinging doors that separated the kitchen from the bar. "I'd get in there if I were you. The lads are telling tales about you to your Da that have got him looking pretty red in the face."

Patrick's first inclination was to turn right around and walk out again in order to escape the razzing he had to look forward to from a pack of flagrant meddlers. Unfortunately he knew there was no escaping the inevitable. "Damn that Sean. He never could keep his mouth shut."

Grimly he started toward the door, then scowled back over his shoulder as Nolan dogged his footsteps. "Where do you think you're going?"

Nolan's ample jowls quivered with his wide smile. "I'm your godfather," he reminded. "Got a right to hear if the devil's been gaining ground when I wasn't looking."

"Good Lord!" Breathing fire, Patrick charged through the swinging doors. "Sean! Just what kind of bull have you been spreading?"

"Who me?" Sean McBride held up his hands as he sidestepped along the edge of the long polished bar. He was almost forty years old, taller and more heavily muscled than Patrick, but his hot-tempered younger brother had never shown much respect for his venerable age or superior size. Come to think of it, neither had Neal or Kevin, who were pushing him forward just as forcefully as he backed away.

"Call him off, Ma," Sean pleaded half-seriously, curling a protective arm in front of the mug of beer he was holding as he noted the violent sparks in his brother's green eyes. "Watch it, fella. This is a new suit."

Molly McBride, a five feet tall redheaded dynamo who had ruled her all-male household with an iron hand, could still command instant obedience even though her sons were all adults and no longer lived at home. She was past sixty, the flaming red in her hair subdued by silver, and her angular features were softened by the passing years, but her eyes were as vivid green as they had been in her youth. They twinkled brightly as she emitted an oft-repeated line, "There'll be no brawling in here. This is a respectable place of business."

Coming around the bar, she placed herself between Patrick and Sean as she'd done many times when they'd been boys. "Now Paddy, pray tell us how you came to be without your clothes in court today." She shot a disapproving frown at her eldest. "We've already heard Sean's thoughts on the matter."

"Yeah, Paddy." Neal, the second oldest at thirty-five, repeated the childish nickname his brother despised as he stepped forward and placed a heavy arm over Patrick's shoulder. "They say the Iron Maiden can flay the skin off an inept attorney, but I never thought they meant it literally. That looks like a nasty bruise you're hiding under your hair."

"I'm not hiding anything," Patrick shot back tersely, unconsciously raising his fingers to his forehead.

"So we heard, little brother," Neal teased as twin dimples went wild in his cheeks. "Tell me, were you cited for contempt before or after you took your clothes off?"

"How did you know I got cited?" Patrick growled, sure that his note to Sean hadn't mentioned the contempt charge.

"My spies are everywhere," Sean announced, then revealed, "Actually, the lady who picked up your suit happened to mention it."

Neal inquired curiously, "Care to relate which parts of your anatomy Judge Cramer liked best?"

"I want to know which one of her discoveries earned Patrick that lump on the head." Sean shrugged as Kevin and Neal's brows shot up to their hairlines. Looking sheepish, he admitted, "Well, I didn't find out everything."

"You idiot," Patrick snapped, "you didn't find out anything!"

"Probably the legs," Sean went on as if Patrick hadn't opened his mouth. "Too hairy and knobby-kneed. Don't you think so, Neal?"

"Don't listen to him, Paddy," Neal advised sympathetically as he gave Patrick another spine-jarring squeeze. "I think you've got great legs."

"Better get this man a beer, Da," Kevin, the youngest McBride brother, suggested as he held out his own empty glass for a refill. "Looks like he'll need help loosening his tongue."

Behind the bar, Thomas McBride hid his grin as he turned away from the family gathering in order to draw two beers. Not a day passed that he didn't wonder how a stout, balding, barrel-chested bartender from the back streets of Dublin had managed to marry such a beautiful woman and father four such remarkable sons. Every one of them had Molly's green eyes and various shades of her glorious red hair. Neal had her dimples. The two youngest, Patrick and Kevin, had inherited her temper, but other than that, they'd taken little else from their mother and absolutely nothing from him.

They were all more than six feet tall, long, lean and muscular. Any one of them could think circles around their father, but to Thomas's relief, none had ever tried. They were fine sons, if overly rambunctious and too smart for their own good. Loving sons, who respected both of their parents. Thomas had demanded they complete their educations, but he'd never expected them all to become lawyers. Every time he thought about the thriving firm of McBride & McBride, founded by Sean and partnered by the other three, he became choked up with pride.

"I hope you didn't swallow Sean's blarney," Patrick said worriedly to his father as he tossed off Neal's arm and slid onto a bar stool. "It wasn't half as ludicrous as it sounds."

"It better not be," Thomas stated sternly, deciding it was time to step in and save Patrick from another round of his brother's grilling. "You can come into the back and tell me about it, Paddy, where we'll be well away from the likes of them hooligans. Molly, can you take my place for a while, darlin'?''

"Whenever did I not?" Molly gave her husband a cheeky grin as she stepped back behind the bar.

"Nolan said you were upset," Patrick said to his father, glaring at his brothers as he picked up his mug and hopped off the stool to follow his father.

"He was just giving you a hard time," Thomas said as he walked along behind the bar on his way to the kitchen. "If you didn't drop your pants to impress a pretty female judge, I won't be upset at all."

"Sean!" Patrick's grip on the mug almost broke the glass.

Sean shook his head, looking innocent. "I don't know where he got that idea. I told him your note said it was your lucky day, not hers."

"I'll get you for this," Patrick groaned under his breath as he passed Sean's stool.

"No need," Sean called after him. "Carla's sent Ryan to her mother's so we can have dinner alone. She's making her famous bouillabaisse."

"Punishment enough," Patrick agreed as he remembered the last time he'd been required to endure his sister-in-law's favorite meal for special occasions.

Twenty minutes later the entire family was seated around a large table in the pub's eating area, drinking a last beer and digesting Patrick's watered-down version of his day's activities. Usually the brothers made plans to have dinner with someone right after leaving their parents' place, but that rarely stopped Molly from foisting platters of batter-fried mushrooms, onion rings and spiced vegetables on them. Patrick was amazed they all didn't look like Nolan, who could eat one french fry and put on five extra pounds.

"After all that, Cramer still ruled in your favor?" Kevin asked as he popped a golden mushroom into his mouth. "Amazing."

"The woman has class," Patrick said, shocking everyone into silence. "What'd I say?"

Molly spoke for the others. "If I remember correctly, the last time you spoke of Blythe Cramer, you called her 'old snoot face.'"

A tinge of red started up Patrick's neck. "Back then we were kids. People change."

"Of course they do, Paddy." Molly reached over and patted Patrick's hand as the male members of the party burst out laughing.

"Can we talk about something else?" Patrick demanded. He'd been roasted on the family spit long enough. It was about time someone else took a turn. Then he glanced at his watch and saw he had to leave if he wanted to change and make it back downtown before seven. "I didn't realize it was so late. I've got a date."

"Hold on." Neal grabbed hold of Patrick's arm before he could get up from the table. "I've got an announcement to make."

"Can't it wait?" Patrick asked impatiently, but sat back down on his chair.

Neal shrugged, his expression deceptively nonchalant. "Yeah, but if I don't tell you now, who knows when I'll work up the courage again. After what you just went through, I can just imagine what my news will bring."

"You provided most of what I just went through," Patrick pointed out sarcastically.

"As your elders, it's our duty to keep you humble," Sean quipped.

"A duty we do not take lightly," Neal agreed.

"Blacken their eyes," Kevin suggested. "I would, but I haven't finished my beer."

Before the brothers got into another slanging match, Molly held up her hand. "Go ahead, Neal," she ordered, sensing his announcement meant more to him than he was letting on. "What is it?"

"Well, Ma," Neal began. "You know how you're always telling us that you should have a whole house full of grandchildren by now?"

Kevin moaned, "I knew it. You may be old but not smart. You've been fooling around with that architect in the next office, and now you're pregnant!" As soon as he said it, he realized that something of the kind might really have happened. "Hey! She's not—"

"Nobody's pregnant!" Neal shook his head in disgust. "As I was saying before I was so rudely interrupted, I think it's about time one of us thought about joining Sean in the blessed state of matrimony."

"You're getting married?" The question was posed collectively by five astonished people.

Neal nodded. "As soon as I can arrange it."

Ever since their high school days, the McBride brothers were considered a scourge on the female population of Columbus. Sean had finally married, but none of the others, who were all past thirty, had shown the slightest inclination to settle down. Indeed, they were very open about their preference for fast cars and fast women to marriage and a sedate family life. The possibility of Neal voluntarily relinquishing his position as a free-wheeling man-about-town was shocking and a mother's dream come true.

Her eyes shining, Molly clamped her hands together over her bosom. "Is she Irish?"

"I don't know." Neal appeared to be slightly puzzled by the question. "I never thought to ask her."

"That's all right," Molly put in hastily. "I don't care what she is as long as she's healthy."

"I'm not buying a horse, Ma." Neal frowned at his mother's statement, knowing exactly where the woman's thoughts were centered. "And I'm not letting Tamarra meet you until you swear you're not going to ask her to open her mouth so you can check out her teeth."

"Tamarra. Hmmm," Molly considered. "That name could be Irish. What do you think, Tom?"

"Could be." Thomas took one look at Neal's flushed face and offered in a conciliatory tone, "But I'm sure we'll love her, no matter what she is. How soon can we meet her? We'll be on our best behavior, won't we, darlin'?"

After Neal agreed to bring Tamarra Wilson to meet the family sometime during the weekend, the discussion became fixed on details of the upcoming wedding. As soon as Patrick had extended his best wishes to Neal, he rose to leave. "I've got to go, Ma, Da. I'm already late."

"A date." Molly recalled his earlier pronouncement. Her tone conveyed hope. "Anyone special?"

Patrick just grinned, and his mother threw up her hands. "I hope you take a page out of your brother's book in the very near future. You're not getting any younger, you know."

"I'll keep that in mind, Ma. See you." Before she could continue, Patrick made a quick exit. Now that Neal had defected, he knew very well who was next in line for his mother's lectures, but he hadn't expected her to start in on him even before his brother's wedding. He wondered what she'd say if he presented Blythe as a possible holder of a future position as his wife. That would take some of the starch out of her.

As he walked outside to his car, Patrick was amazed with himself for even imagining such a thing. He'd never come close to proposing marriage to any woman, let alone one who'd need dynamite to pry the silver spoon out of her mouth far enough for him to kiss her. Blythe Cramer and Molly McBride would have nothing in common. Still, it would be interesting to watch the two of them together.

As far as he knew, other than seeing them at school on parents' night once or twice, Blythe knew nothing about his folks. The McBrides had lived in a middle-class house on the edge of a fancy neighborhood, but Blythe had grown up on a mammoth estate. It had always surprised Patrick that her parents hadn't sent her off to some elite private school. He couldn't count the times he'd wished that she'd transfer out of the district.

Since the first grade, they'd been in constant competition. He'd avoided her, considering her not only a "rich bitch" but also a "nice girl"—a type he didn't have much time for. Even so, he'd kept close track of her career and had a healthy respect for what she'd managed to accomplish, though the odds had been stacked heavily against her. He'd always thought her beautiful, though he wouldn't have admitted it to a soul. He supposed he'd been guilty of stereotyping her and had never quite dared to cross the line between their two worlds.

Today he'd decided to take that dare. Patrick slid behind the wheel of his used Alfa Romeo Spyder, turned the key and gunned the engine. He wheeled down the small city street, heading for the freeway.

"Look out, Ms. Cramer," he warned as he stepped on the gas and shot into the fast lane. "I've raised my battle flag, and I'm going to take you by storm."

Four

It was almost seven-thirty when Blythe arrived at André's. She hoped Patrick didn't think she'd come late on purpose, or suspect that the black scoop-necked sheath she had on hadn't come out of the closet in her office. He didn't need to know she'd rushed home at five o'clock, taken a bubble bath, fixed her hair and changed clothes half a dozen times before deciding on the sleeveless silk.

Nor was she willing to admit that she hadn't chosen the dress because of the hot July weather, but because it clung to all the right curves and shimmered in all the right places. She kept telling herself that it was an understated black dress, perfect for going out to dinner with a professional colleague.

"What's your excuse?" sounded a familiar voice from behind her before she pulled open the door to the restaurant.

Blythe bristled for a second, then laughed when she turned around, noting the wind-blown condition of Patrick's wavy hair and the harried expression on his face. "I got so immersed in tomorrow's caseload I lost track of the time."

"That's a good one." He nodded his approval of her smooth delivery, thinking her explanation could have been the truth, but guessing it was a lie.

Blythe's makeup was perfect. Soft smoke above her beguiling blue eyes, shaded pink blush to emphasize her high cheekbones, a brush of rose on rosebud lips, all expertly applied. Tiny diamond studs offset her delicate earlobes, and not one glossy black hair on her head was out of place.

She looked too good, too finished, to have just come up from the depths of a stack of thick legal briefs. Patrick's green eyes twinkled at the thought that she had dressed up for the occasion—for him. "I got tied up in traffic."

"Uh-huh." Blythe lifted her shoulders and smiled. If he had gotten stuck in a traffic jam, he couldn't have sweated it out too long. His hair was a bit more mussed than usual, but the white collar of his button-down oxford was crisp, his thin-striped silk tie secured in a tight Windsor knot, and his gray pin-striped suit was without a wrinkle. "That excuse is a bit trite, but it generally works."

"No more trite than yours." Patrick grinned and shrugged as he took hold of her arm to escort her inside. His fingers curved over the soft, smooth skin. Touching her was pure erotic torture.

Patrick drew in a quick breath before his eyes struggled up from her body and settled down warmly on her lips. *God, the things I could do to that mouth.* "Shall

we skip drinks at the bar and go straight in to dinner?''
His tone was silky and smooth, matching the sensual
images her little nothing of a dress incited in his mind.

''Fine with me,'' Blythe said, but her words came out
a bit too husky for her liking. How was she ever going
to make it through the evening if he kept looking at her
like that? As if he'd not only like to skip drinks, but
dinner too, and anything else that stood between them
and the nearest bed? How was she going to stand it, if
he continued to caress her with that voice, spoken in
tones that emoted sex with every syllable?

Being out with him was just buying trouble. As much
as she hated to admit it, she had spent most of her day
thinking about that night in the tenth grade when he'd
kissed her, when she'd felt the brush of his fingers on
the upper curve of her breast. She couldn't help but
wonder what it would be like if he kissed her again,
touched her. What it would be like if they...

''Who invited all these people?'' Patrick growled
when his eyes became adjusted to the light inside the
dark restaurant. ''I chose this place for its...''

''Yes?'' Blythe invited, her blue eyes daring him to
admit what they both knew to be true. At some point
during the day, Patrick had decided she should be the
next in a long line of women to suffer from the hallu-
cinatory virus he and his brothers were famous for
spreading around town. The ''now you see 'em, now
you don't'' McBride malady wasn't fatal, but left scars,
and if she could help it, she wouldn't become another
member of the walking wounded, no matter what her
body wanted.

Moreover, she'd be wise to remember that Patrick
might not be above taking unfair advantage of her. If
he did hope to persuade her into bed with an offer to

keep quiet about this morning's episode, she couldn't afford to let him know how attractive she found him. Her fantasies about him would just have to be content to stay in her head.

"I chose André's for the good food," Patrick concluded innocently. "I was just hoping we could enjoy a quiet meal together. We have a lot to talk about."

"We do?" Blythe couldn't quite keep the suspicion out of her voice.

Patrick frowned at the question he saw in her eyes. "I thought we could spend the next couple of hours catching up on each other's activities since college. We've never been friends exactly, but we are more than passing acquaintances."

"I suppose arch rivals could be considered more than passing acquaintances," Blythe allowed thoughtfully and couldn't resist smiling at his black scowl. "Ready to brave the crowd?"

"I am if you are."

The dimly lit foyer was packed with people coming and going from the piano bar and dining room. Patrick stepped behind Blythe, placing his hands on her shoulders as she led the way toward the reservation stand. Pressing himself close, Patrick breathed in the scent of roses and knew that, whatever her excuse, he would have waited hours for her to arrive, just so he could enjoy her scent once again.

"Does your skin always smell like this, or do you bathe in rose petals? I've always wondered," he whispered in her ear, but regretted his curiosity when he felt her stiffen.

"I'm sure I didn't hear that." Blythe couldn't think of any other answer that wouldn't be as provocative as his question. If a woman didn't want Patrick McBride to take a mile, she couldn't give an inch, and Blythe was already having a hard time controlling an urge to be generous.

"I'm sure I didn't ask a proper judge such an improper question," Patrick retorted, giving Blythe's shoulders a very unrepentant squeeze.

Blythe was glad she had her back to him. If he had intended this dinner to place them on a more personal footing, he'd already succeeded without half trying. The feel of his hands on her shoulders made her skin tingle. She wasn't fifteen any longer, and knew exactly what that response meant. Unfortunately Patrick would, too, and she wasn't prepared to trust him with that kind of knowledge. She was going to have to be very careful.

With reluctance Patrick dropped his hands as they reached the maître d'. "Reservations for Patrick McBride and Blythe Cramer," he said, grinning widely as he emphasized the order of their names.

Blythe couldn't help but laugh. "One for you, counselor."

"Took me long enough," Patrick muttered comically under his breath as they both followed the maître d'.

They were seated in a plush pale blue velvet banquette in a rear corner of the large dining room. The curved, high back gave them some measure of privacy from other diners, and the low lighting made the setting seem far more intimate than Blythe would have liked. When Patrick slid in beside her, it was all Blythe could do not to edge farther away.

To her surprise, the first thing he ordered was a bottle of champagne. She'd never thought of him as a champagne person, let alone a connoisseur of fine wines, but he seemed very familiar with all brands on the list, and his pronunciation was perfect.

Once he'd tasted the choice he'd made, and Blythe's glass was poured, he settled back on the seat and looked at her. "You could at least try not to look so stunned. Besides, I really haven't changed all that much over the years, just picked up some finesse. I soon discovered that when dating a high-society type, a man must familiarize himself with the correct and fashionable means to ply her with liquor. I could hardly seduce you with Ripple. You'd have turned up your lovely nose."

"I don't seduce easy, McBride, even with champagne," Blythe warned calmly, hiding the irritation she felt at being labeled a high-society type and his intimation that she was a snob.

"Too bad. Well, at least I've proved my point."

"What's that?"

"That I've lost some of the rough edges I had in high school." He continued, "What you see before you now is a sophisticated man of the world who can play in any league."

"So I've heard," she stated pointedly.

"Been checking up on me, have you?" Patrick inquired. "Now that's interesting."

"I have not been checking up on you," Blythe gritted through clenched teeth, trying hard not to lose her temper. She hadn't been checking up on him—not exactly. After all, she read the newspapers. She'd heard the courthouse gossip. She'd kept up some of her high school friendships, and Patrick's name had come up a time or two. She hadn't sought any knowledge about him. It had been dropped in her lap.

"Turnabout is only fair play," Patrick admonished, enjoying the blue sparks that flickered in her eyes. "I've accumulated a wealth of information about you over the years. I guess in the back of my mind I always knew we'd meet again, and I wanted to be prepared.''

Blythe shook her head. What exactly had he been preparing for? What was going on in the back of his mind right now? Did he hope to undermine her election by pressing her to have an affair with an outspoken liberal? ''What's really going on here, McBride?'' she asked on a long sigh. ''Why this sudden interest in me? What are you after?''

Molten green eyes told her exactly what he was after, but when he spoke, his words were pleasant and easy, edged with only the slightest amount of sensual undertone. ''For starters, I want us to be... friends.''

''I can't think why.'' Blythe shifted uncomfortably on the seat, placing a few more inches between them.

''Then don't think—no matter how that goes against your conservative grain—just feel. Trust me. It'll do you a world of good.''

''It will, huh?''

''You do tend to be a bit stuffy, Cramer.''

''And you tend to be insufferable, McBride.''

''A match made in heaven. To us.'' Patrick saluted her with his glass, the grooves in his cheeks mocking her hesitation to follow suit. ''Come on, Cramer. I'm only making a friendly toast, not asking for a lifelong commitment. Loosen up.''

''To friends, wherever they might be.'' Blythe nodded, took a small sip of the excellent champagne, then set down her glass. She was growing more and more confused by this thrust-and-parry game Patrick was playing with her. She couldn't understand what he was trying to accomplish. Politically they were on opposite sides of the fence. Getting involved would do neither of them any good. Couldn't he see that? Maybe he didn't want to see that.

"Okay, McBride. Let's lay our cards on the table," Blythe suggested as soon as the waiter had taken their dinner order. "Professionally we work opposite sides of the bar. Personally we can't stand each other, and politically we'll never see eye to eye, so what's the point of this dinner?"

Patrick digested the cut-and-dried quality of her speech, trying to decide if she was deliberately being obtuse or if she was truly that scared of her own feelings. Every time they made eye contact, it was like setting a torch to dry grass. Whenever he touched her, he felt as if he were about to go up in smoke, and a blind man could tell she felt the same. "If you feel that way, Blythe, why did you accept my invitation?"

"The truth?"

Patrick didn't like the sound of that question and sensed he was about to hear something he liked even less. "Truth being you were desperate for my charming company?"

"Hardly."

Patrick took a deep breath, leaned back and gave her a ridiculously endearing smile. "Then I don't want to hear it. Ignorance is bliss. I would just as soon go on believing that what happened in court today was the start of something beautiful."

Blythe gasped as he lifted her hand from her lap to the table. He massaged the tightly clenched fingers with the pad of his thumb, until they opened to reveal her soft palm. "See?"

"See what?" Blythe could barely get the words out, her eyes glued to the erotic motion of his thumb as it stroked her palm. Her small hand was cradled in the warm curve of his, and her fingers trembled with the sensual message his tender caress imprinted on her mind.

"Like it or not, everything in you wants to open to me," he said huskily. "You just need more convincing."

"No!" Blythe snatched her hand out of his grasp. Her whole body felt hot, inflamed by the images his words conveyed. When he shifted on the velvet seat and his thigh came into contact with hers, she jerked away as if she'd been burned.

Desperation inspired the scorn in her voice when she demanded, "Convince me you're not out to make another conquest, McBride. Convince me you won't resort to blackmail when your usual methods fail."

Patrick narrowed his eyes on her stormy features, confused by the accusation in her eyes. "Blackmail? Coercion by threat? All I did was hold your hand, Cramer. Even you can't be that repressed."

"Oh!" Blythe was grateful for the insult. It served to release all restraint. They were in a public place, so she couldn't raise her voice, but intensity made up for any lack of volume. "If you think I'm repressed because I'm concerned for my public image, then I'm repressed and glad of it. I'd much rather have that label than the one you deserve, if I'm proved right."

"Proved right about what?"

"Are you running for a seat in the House next election?"

"What!" Patrick exclaimed, not caring that his loud outburst drew several curious stares from other patrons.

"Are you?"

"So what if I am? Would that make me a criminal?"

"Of course not."

"Then what are you saying? You can't afford to be seen with one of my kind? Is the Republican party that intimidated by the opposition? If so, maybe you should consider switching sides and rid yourself of this stupid paranoia." Patrick was more than a little irritated by the hostile turn in the conversation. One minute they were sharing champagne and exchanging playful gibes, and the next she was accusing him of God knows what.

"From what I've seen and heard from you tonight, I don't think I'm being paranoid at all. Wouldn't my political opponents just love to find out what went on between us today? I told you today how the headlines might read. 'Crusader for Justice Conked Out by Contemptuous Judge.'"

A chuckle came out of Patrick's mouth before he could prevent it. He shook his head, sighing indulgently. "So that's what this is all about. You don't have to worry, Blythe. I'd never let the press crucify the lady in my life, even if she is a Republican."

Viewing the continued mistrust in her eyes, Patrick held up his hand and swore, "Honest, Your Honor. I wouldn't do that to you."

"In other words, as your mistress, I'll never have to worry about such a story leaking to the press," Blythe clarified his position in a smooth tone, all the while praying he wouldn't confirm her worst suspicions. She would prefer to go through the rest of her life without acquiring proof that Patrick McBride wasn't worth a single one of her fantasies.

"You wound me," Patrick complained half-seriously. It was clear she didn't trust him any further than she could throw him, and that bothered him a lot. Then he realized what else she'd said, and he couldn't get the words out fast enough. "If you become my mistress, I'll do nothing to besmirch your honor."

Blythe offered a weak smile at his pun, too caught up in the trap she was laying to applaud his clever choice of wording. "Then so long as we're lovers, I can trust in your loyalty?"

"Definitely," Patrick agreed, amazed at how much ground was being covered without him pushing for it. Somewhere in the back of his mind, he felt a twinge of something akin to disappointment, but he ignored it. For Blythe, he would happily forgo the excitement of the chase for the heady thrill of victory.

"Do you see this as a short-term or long-term affair?" Blythe inquired with apparent calm, but inside she was seething. Beneath the table she twisted her linen napkin as viciously as she would have liked to twist Patrick's neck.

To cover his astonishment at the question, Patrick took a gulp of champagne. Their food arrived before he had to respond, and he was extremely grateful for the diversion. He had to do some fast readjusting to his thinking. He'd thought Blythe repressed, and here she was, very matter-of-factly eliminating any emotional issues that might stand in the way of their having an affair. She was not only trying to determine the depth, but the length of their forthcoming involvement.

In one way, he was glad he wouldn't have to devote a lot of time convincing her they were meant for each other. But in another, he regretted her worldliness. Not enough to prevent him from taking her up on her offer, true, but still, it would have been nice if she was as new to this kind of arrangement as he was.

For the first time in his life, he was after more than a one-night stand. He was offering long-term commitment, even considering marriage. Did she feel the same way, or was he just the next in a number of discreet little affairs she'd conducted over the years? Who had tutored her in this cosmopolitan approach to matters of the heart? He didn't think he could stand finding out.

A short-term or long-term affair, she wanted to know. Patrick almost felt as if she were asking him for a judicial decision based on past precedents, rather than an emotional one based on gut-wrenching feeling. Had she changed so much from the sweet innocent he'd known in high school? Evidently she had.

Once the waiter had served their dishes and left them alone, Patrick responded to her question, attempting to emulate her cool manner, though he could feel his desire for her searing through him. "Our involvement will have to be long-term, Blythe. What I feel for you won't end overnight."

Blythe stared into his eyes for a long time, saying nothing.

Patrick smiled in relief. All the passion and fire he could hope for was there in her eyes. All the emotion that was lacking in her words was revealed in their turbulent blue depths.

"What I feel for you won't be quenched overnight, either," Blythe said softly, then opened up with both barrels. "You're a first rate scumbucket, McBride, as addicted to liberal sex as you are to liberal politics. Well, I'm not playing or paying. I won't go to bed with you to keep my name out of the papers."

Slowly and deliberately she lifted her glass of champagne and threw the contents into his face. Before he knew what had hit him, she had moved around to the opposite side of the booth and was on her feet.

"I've always heard champagne is the best thing for drowning your sorrows," she tossed airily over her shoulder as she left him.

In less than five minutes Blythe was inside her car and driving down High Street. She was only five miles from her apartment, which was located in the near-north side of town. The drive seemed to take less time than usual; she was so angry she wasn't aware of how fast she was going. Later, she would give thanks that no patrol car had pulled her over for speeding. Even the smallest indiscretion on her part was subject to public scrutiny.

She parked her car in the private space allocated to her in the lot and muttered angrily to herself every step of the way up the sidewalk. She was halfway through the security doors of her building before she was hit broadside by six feet of Irish dander in human form. She was whisked through the door in two seconds and off her feet in two more.

One hand clutched like a vise around each of Blythe's arms, Patrick held her at eye level. Nose to nose, he growled, "Do you want to continue this fight in your apartment or go two out of three falls out here?"

"Put me down, you...you...ow!" Blythe bit her tongue when she landed, teetered out of balance and fell against Patrick's chest. "Let go of me," she commanded as her fingers clutched the lapels of his suit, and she buried her face in his shirt.

Patrick pulled her off him by the scruff of the neck as if she were a spitting kitten. His fingers wound in the silky hair at her nape, he waited patiently for her to right herself, and impatiently for an answer to his challenge. When she tried to slap his face, he tugged on her hair. "I'm warning you, Cramer. We either take this inside, or you're going down for the count!"

Blythe sputtered and shook with the force of her rage, but realized she was up against someone with an even bigger temper than her own. If it were possible, smoke would be coming out of Patrick's ears to match the explosive anger she saw in his eyes.

"Fine!" She charged down the hall, her head held high, her back straight, as Patrick stalked after her.

In the elevator her eyes dared him to take up where they'd left off, but he remained silent, a killing silence that shook her to the core. This was not the reaction of a man who'd just proven himself to be the lowest of the low, it was the response of one who'd been unjustly accused of a reprehensible crime.

Was that it? Had she made a mistake? Was it possible she'd misjudged him? No. She'd given him every opportunity to prove himself, and he'd ignored each one. He'd condemned himself with his own words.

Patrick pressed his spine into the wall, keeping himself as far away from Blythe as he could. If she were a man, she'd already have two black eyes, but he'd never hit a woman in his life. He stared at her mouth, wondering how she'd look without teeth.

She deserved a good pop, and by the time he would be finished with her, she'd be sorry he wouldn't settle for something that quick. No matter what she thought, the reason he'd come after her had nothing to do with thwarted male ego. She'd attacked something far more elemental—wounded an essential part of him—his integrity.

His honor had never been questioned, not by anyone, and the thought that she believed him capable of guaranteeing his silence with her sexual favors was impossible to take. He wouldn't take it! Not even from her, the woman he wanted, the woman he had always wanted.

It was ironic. He'd admitted to himself that Blythe had placed a long-ago claim on his heart, that he had been hers for a great many years, just moments before she'd stomped on everything he stood for. Apparently, what he felt for her had never been mutual. To counteract the pain that knowledge gave him, Patrick clenched his hands until the knuckles turned white.

"Lay one finger on me, and I'll have you jailed before the first bruise sets in," Blythe blustered, gulping down fear as she watched the sporadic motions of his fists.

The elevator door slid open as he spoke from behind her. "First blackmail, now assault. Believe me, lady, if I were capable of either, you'd be my first choice as victim."

"I've been victimized quite enough for one day, thank you," Blythe retorted defensively as she inserted her key and pushed open the door of her apartment. She switched on the lights, then turned back to gesture Patrick inside.

Patrick's expression was skeptical as he strode past her. He stood for a moment on the polished white marble flooring of the entry and looked around. Then his curiosity drew him into the large living room.

The long rectangular space was perfect, antiseptically, ascetically, artificially perfect. White on white, the low cushioned sofa and chairs, chrome and glass tables and plush carpeting were an interior designer's dream. Mauve and gray walls conveyed the only warmth in the room. Art deco paintings, the only life.

Patrick's anger died as he surveyed his surroundings. The woman he wanted wouldn't be happy in a room like this. Evidently he'd misjudged the present-day Blythe Cramer as much as she'd misjudged him. What did he care what the coldhearted woman who resided here thought of him or his sterling character? His eyes bleak, he took a last lingering look before taking his leave.

It was then that he spotted a few things he'd missed on first notice. Some crewel embroidered pillows were scattered on the couch, and a paperback book was stuffed between the white cushions. One corner of a multicolored crocheted afghan peeped out from beneath a nearby chair. A fuzzy pink slipper lay upside down under a glass table.

"Very modern and elegant. Did you design this room yourself?" he asked, hoping she wouldn't sense the importance he attached to the question.

"A daughter of a friend who's majoring in interior decoration did this room," Blythe replied uncertainly. She preferred his curiosity to his anger, but wasn't the least bit prepared for the sudden switch. "I . . . eh . . . I don't spend a lot of time here, so I gave her free license to do what she liked. It's not really my style but . . . Where are you going?"

"Aha!" Patrick pronounced with gleeful satisfaction from somewhere inside her bedroom. "Now this is more like it. Antique furniture, a ton of books and a soft, comfy bed." He ran a hand over the knubby texture of the crocheted spread then looked up through the matching tester that sheltered it, imagining the interesting patterns of light her small bedside lamp would throw up on the ceiling. He could picture Blythe curled up against a bank of pillows within the wispy shelter of the bed, reading one of the books from the wall of filled shelves. He could also see himself, right beside her. They wouldn't read long.

"Patrick McBride, you come out of there right now," Blythe called imperiously. "You had something to say when you came in, so kindly say it, then get out of my apartment."

"Right," she heard him mutter, and she took a wary step backward as he added menacingly, "I've got a mouthful to say, and you're going to listen."

When he reentered the room, Patrick didn't try to head her off at the door, but sauntered toward the couch. He shrugged out of his suit coat, tossed it over the back of the couch, then plopped himself down on the cushions. Showing a marked indifference for the immaculate polish of the glass, he placed his feet up on the coffee table. He tugged off his tie and threw it on the floor.

"What this room needs is a man's touch," he proclaimed stoutly. "It would take me ten seconds to mess it up to the point where it would be livable."

"Is that what you came up here to say?" Blythe countered, completely baffled by the myriad of behavioral changes she'd witnessed in the space of two minutes. "What happened to all that righteous indignation you were displaying downstairs?"

"Ah, yes." Patrick patted the cushion beside him. "Come here, Cramer. Before we proceed any further, we're going to set a few things straight."

Five

Blythe glared at the man who was seated on her couch and looked for all the world as if he were the master of all he surveyed—the room, all its furniture and her. He'd even commanded her to sit down beside him as if she were a royal lap dog being called to heel by the resident monarch.

"There *is* one thing we need to set straight, McBride," she said, in complete accord with him on the first part of his maddening statement. "You've got some colossal nerve coming in here and ordering me around."

"Nerves of steel," Patrick quipped and chuckled at her outraged expression. "To take what you dished out tonight without doing you great bodily harm is irrefutable proof that I'm made of pretty strong stuff." He shot her a roguish grin. "You should be glad of that, Cramer, not angry."

Abruptly Blythe found that the laughing, green-eyed, six foot leprechaun who took great pleasure in raising her Irish often was just too hard to resist. All she could do was shake her head in defeat. "I pity the poor soul who ends up with you, McBride," she muttered wearily as she walked to the couch and perched herself warily at the opposite end from him. "You really are too much."

"Not for you," Patrick returned softly, watching her. "When you find out that my motives toward you are strictly honorable, you'll realize that I'm perfect for you, just as I've come to understand how perfect you are for me. That's the only logical conclusion you'll be able to reach."

"I'm too tired to play games, McBride." Blythe forced herself to lean back against the cushions. "Just say what you really came here to say, and let me draw my own conclusions. If a lawyer has a good defense, he doesn't need to lead the witness."

"Fair enough." Patrick held up his hand and declared, "I, Patrick McBride, am not now, nor have I ever contemplated running for public office. I have and always will find greater satisfaction in winning unpopular cases than popular votes. I have absolutely no intention of giving up my private practice. I love what I'm doing and can't see a time when I won't."

He waited for that to sink in and nodded smugly when he saw that it had.

His attitude might be insufferable, but Blythe knew in her heart that Patrick wasn't lying. She'd completely misjudged him. No wonder he'd been so angry. "Then you didn't—"

"No."

"And you weren't planning to—"

"Oh, I was planning to all right, but only if you were just as eager as I. We almost set your office on fire this morning, Cramer. I don't know about you, but I haven't felt that kind of heat since a certain night in tenth grade. I had no intention of letting another decade pass before doing something about it. My motive for asking you out was as simple as that."

"Oh." Blythe gulped, feeling as if she were still that teenage girl who hadn't known how to handle all the feelings that a much younger but just as potent Patrick had created. "I...eh...it looks like I might have leaped to some very wrong conclusions."

"Very wrong," Patrick responded.

"Then I apologize."

"As well you should," Patrick declared rather pompously. "You're just lucky you didn't falsely accuse a man with a less forgiving nature than myself. You, Your Honor, have been found guilty of defamation of character, slander, mental torture, emotional abuse, and worst of all..." He eyed the still-damp stains on his shoulders. "The ruination of another one of my best suits."

Blythe rolled her eyes and stared at the ceiling. "Good grief."

Patrick grinned. He reached over and took her hand, gratified when she made no effort to pull away. He tugged gently, and Blythe willingly moved closer. Smiling down into her face, he asked, "So where did you ever get the cockeyed idea I was planning to run for a seat in the House?"

Blythe was loath to admit how much credence she, a judge, had given to hearsay and rumor. Even so, she couldn't quite bring herself to lie. After clearing her throat, she conceded, "That's the latest word on the courthouse grapevine."

"Oh, Blythe."

With those two simple words, Patrick conveyed the depth of his disappointment in her. Blythe felt worse than if he'd launched into a blistering Celtic tirade. She had realized over the past few minutes that Patrick's respect was something she wanted. They had always been equals on every possible level and she didn't want that to change.

She couldn't have Patrick McBride thinking she was a paranoid coward who felt threatened by every piece of gossip put forth by her political opponents. "With all the grilling I've endured by the press since my appointment, I've had to be careful," she began in her defense. "If some reporter had gotten wind of what happened in my court today, seen you bleeding all over the place, those who want me out of office would have had a field day. And what better man to bring down a conservative foe than the 'Columbus Crusader'?"

"That's just a stupid nickname. I've been called that ever since I kept a ninety-year-old grandmother out of jail for stealing food. Any public defender would have done the same."

"Not necessarily. You've made quite a name for yourself, McBride, and as far as I know, it's deserved. I've followed your career, and that's probably why I found it so easy to believe you'd soon be a candidate for some political office. You've got what it takes."

"Considering the fact you also thought me capable of sexual coercion, I'm not sure that's a compliment."

Blythe flushed a deep red. "I don't think that anymore."

"Well, I am capable of that and much more," Patrick confessed, intrigued. He loved Blythe's delectable blush and had thought of it often over the years. She'd be amazed and probably extremely annoyed to find out how much he relished the thought of bringing it about again.

Knowing how conservative she was, he couldn't resist saying, "Champagne, candlelight, gourmet food served in a romantic setting. I was trying my best to coerce you into seeing me as your lover. And if that didn't work, I was going to drag you off somewhere and make love to you until you just had to see things my way."

"McBride!" Blythe pressed herself into the corner of the couch, but with one controlled movement of his thigh, Patrick made sure she couldn't get up. He was sitting so close she could feel the vital magnetism that no woman could ignore. She could smell the scent of his cologne and could see the darkened intensity in his eyes. "I . . . I'm not—"

Patrick traced the quivering outline of her protesting mouth with the tip of his finger. "No woman has ever aroused me the way you do, Judge Cramer. That sexy judicial robe you had on today drove me half out of my mind, especially after I knew you wore next to nothing underneath. It was even more provocative than that red silk thing you had on the last time I got close enough to touch you."

Blythe's body quivered as he delicately cupped her breast. She felt the shock from her head to her toes, yet couldn't pull away. Her frantic blue eyes focused on his face but couldn't move away from his mouth. How would it feel to have those lips on hers? To feel his tongue . . . "No! You can't—"

"Can't what? Can't kiss you?" Patrick asked gently. "But you want me to, Blythe. You want me to so much that your eyes mirror nothing but my mouth."

Blythe gasped at the truth, her eyes flying upward just as his mouth descended to give her what she craved. It took less than a second for her to admit that she'd wanted this to happen for more years than she cared to think about. Even so, she gave a tiny moan of surprise as Patrick broke through her natural reserve and unleashed a feminine hunger kept under strict control.

Acting on the fantasies she'd had of this man, Blythe reached up and put her arms around Patrick's neck. Her fingers dove into the thick auburn waves of his hair as she held his head in place for the pleasure of her mouth. She tasted him as she had longed to all day, tasted the wildness and adventure, the easy laughter and roguish charm that was Patrick McBride. With each thrilling probe of his demanding tongue, she grew more reckless. With each brush of his fingers on her taut breasts, she shed another layer of her normal caution.

Patrick tried to hold on to his control, tried to ignore the ache in his loins, but his body refused to comply with the civilized dictates of his brain. His imagination had lied. Kissing Blythe wasn't sweet loving pleasure. It was pure heavenly torture. The tiniest movement of her lips, the smallest stroking of her tongue, and he was tormented by an overpowering need to be inside her. He wanted her naked, no inch of her creamy skin left untouched by his eyes, his hands, his lips.

He'd been told that he was an expert lover, but he was no match for this woman. One touch of her hands in his hair, the feel of her breasts against his chest, and he forgot to think, couldn't remember any techniques he knew most pleasured a woman. He was all hands with no brain, a carnal male without any finesse.

In another minute he wouldn't care whether she wanted it or not, he would have to take her. And if he did, it would be the last time he ever got to touch her. That couldn't happen. He couldn't let that happen.

"Oh, God!" Patrick groaned, wrenching his mouth away from temptation. When he could think enough to talk, he said, "And you say I'm too much! You're incredible, lady. This is incredible."

With one arm, he levered himself to a safer position on the couch, leaned his head back on the cushions and gulped for air. He was trembling with need, shaking like a boy with his first woman. "Dammit! I've been afraid of this all along. A man kisses you, and look what happens to him. Now I know why I never tried anything with you before now."

Blythe didn't react to his evident arousal, but to the derision she heard in his voice. She should never have given her passion free rein. Never! She shouldn't have kissed him as if she never wanted to stop. Now he thought she was some kind of insatiable man-eater. Humiliation overwhelmed her, fueled by the remnants of her damaged pride.

She jumped up from the couch. "I never gave you the chance to try anything with me before, and you needn't be afraid I ever will again! Whatever you think, I'm not the kind of woman who... I never would've..."

Too angry to think straight, she lifted a pillow off the couch and slung it at him. "I don't have to defend my actions to you. Now get out!"

Patrick was stunned by her attack and astonished at the violent temper evidenced by the missile launched at his head. He managed to dodge the pillow but couldn't elude the excitement he felt in the pit of his stomach. The cool, calm, collected facade Blythe Cramer always wore hid as many delightfully arousing things as did her judicial black robes.

At the restaurant, considering what she'd believed about him, she'd shown remarkable restraint. Her accusations had dripped with icy contempt, only her stormy blue eyes revealed any deeper emotion. She'd tossed a glass of champagne into his face to make a point, not because she'd been overcome with outrage. It was the thought that she'd overwhelmed him with the strength of her passion that had accomplished that.

He was going to have such a grand time teaching her how much he enjoyed being overwhelmed. It was only fair. She'd taught him a thing or two tonight. In fact, if they were keeping score, she was well ahead.

"Will you please leave?" Blythe insisted. She couldn't stand the way he was looking at her, not for one more second. He made her feel too vulnerable; he'd stripped away all her sophisticated trappings and located the woman beneath.

Until tonight, until Patrick, no man had melted down the frozen shell that camouflaged her fiery nature. He had managed it with one scorching kiss. Why? she asked herself. Why did it have to be Patrick who blasted through all the barriers she'd so carefully built up? The one man who would take such vengeful joy in the accomplishment?

"You know something, Cramer?" Patrick said, making no move to vacate the premises. "Tonight you taught me a very fundamental lesson about the male of the species. Do you want to hear what it is?"

"No." Blythe made a futile pointing gesture with her arm, knowing full well that Patrick wasn't going to budge until he'd taken his pound of flesh. "All I want to hear is the sound of that door closing behind you."

"I know," he observed softly. "And you know it's not going to happen, not yet, anyway."

Blythe did know, and the bitterness and resignation in her eyes was as apparent as the weakness in her limbs. She sank back down on the couch, wishing she were anywhere but in the same room with Patrick McBride. Striving to maintain her fragile hold on dignity, she crossed her arms over her chest and faced him directly. "Well?"

"You're so beautiful, Blythe," Patrick muttered gruffly. "I don't know if I can look at you and admit this sort of thing without turning into that blithering fool you tossed a pillow at a few moments ago."

He scanned her pale face, the overbright blue eyes, the rose-petal cheeks and the mouth a man would die for. "Then again, when you're angry you don't seem to notice what being near you does to me. To keep my ego intact, I just might have to make you angry most of the time."

"What?" Blythe squeaked in astonishment.

Patrick took a deep breath, then let it out slowly. "I hate to point out the unbecoming tendency you have to jump to the wrong conclusions, sweetheart, but you've done it again. I wasn't making fun of your wonderful responses to me. I was too terrified by my own reactions to consider how you might feel about yours."

"You . . . you were what?"

"Frightened, scared, petrified," Patrick confirmed with a halfhearted smile. "All you had to do was kiss me, and I immediately reverted to that adolescent nit-wit you had to dance with in the tenth grade, the one who almost passed out after one look at your bare breast. I had to hold you that tight to keep myself from falling flat on my face."

He gave a disgusted snort. "And now, after spouting off to you about how much I had changed, what a sophisticated man of the world I've become, I feel like a prize idiot. One lousy kiss, and I'm practically frothing at the mouth, acting on base instinct like the lowest form of life."

Blythe stared at him, at a complete loss for words. His expression was overly tragic, his words tongue-in-cheek, but she sensed he really had felt that way during their kiss, really did think his very obvious, very primitive need for her had turned her off. Considering her eager response, how could he have thought that? Well, why not? She'd thought the same of him.

Patrick held up his hands and lowered his head as if to hide his shame. "I know. I know. A supposedly worldly, civilized man helpless in the throes of primitive lust is not a pretty sight. You're probably so disgusted you'll never let me near you again, and I couldn't blame you."

Blythe couldn't help it. She burst out laughing, at herself and the impossible man who delivered such self-effacing honesty, tender compassion and heady compliments almost in the same breath. Grateful to him for making light of a painful situation, she chided him, "You're the first man to call my kisses lousy, McBride."

Patrick's brows went up as his mouth turned down. "Jeez. There's no doubt about it: I'm still that crude, insensitive jock you knew back in high school. I'll never get a decent woman to look twice at me."

Blythe snuggled back on the cushions, looked at him—more than twice. She heard his intake of breath as she made an inch by inch study of the long, muscular legs thrust beneath her glass coffee table. Leisurely her eyes traveled up the pressed inseam of his gray trousers, lingered at the thin black leather belt around his trim waist, then paused heatedly at every button on his crisp white shirt. "Yup. You're still a jock, McBride, but I've been told I'm a decent woman, and I'm still looking."

Patrick cleared his throat. She was really something. "Then you wouldn't mind if I kissed you again? You're willing to risk what might happen?"

"We decent women understand male weaknesses," she replied loftily. "Of course, we'd never admit it—most unladylike you understand—but occasionally, we've even been known to suffer some very indelicate feelings ourselves whilst in a man's embrace. I am prepared to endure, if I must."

"I think you must, Blythe," Patrick warned thickly as he reached out and pulled her across his lap. "I think we both must."

And it was an endurance contest between two extremely well-matched competitors. Their lips came together with an urgency even greater than before, their bodies clamoring for the feel of the other. As their tongues warred, explored, caressed, neither could declare victory and neither surrendered.

Blythe fought to keep her rising needs in perspective, but very quickly she was all yearning, all give. She drew Patrick to her with her mouth, her hands, the softness of her body, and he took with equal measure. How long had she waited for a man who would whirl her away to a place without convention, a place of unrestricted freedom where all she had to do was feel? How long had she known that man would be Patrick? An hour? A day? Or had she always known?

Patrick tried to think but found all his senses swirling. There wasn't a single part of her that wasn't intoxicating, her scent, her touch, her taste. The shiny ebony strands of her hair encircled his fingers in possessive rings, her fragrant skin claimed him, her soft hands marked him as hers. How had he ever lived so long without this? How could he exist a second longer without more?

A low sound started in his throat, but before he lifted his mouth from hers, he forced himself not to beg. "I can't stop. I don't want to stop. Do you?"

"I can't stop, either," Blythe whispered. "Even if I wanted to."

As Patrick stood up with her in his arms, Blythe couldn't ever remember feeling so much a woman, a woman who knew exactly what she wanted and exactly what she was going to get. The short trip to her bedroom gave her no time for second thoughts, for Patrick filled her mind with suggestions of how it would be when they came together.

When he pulled down her bedspread and set her on the cool sheets, she wouldn't allow him to leave her even long enough to strip off his clothes. She did that for him, challenging him with lambent blue eyes and gasping as he met the challenge. Within seconds they were both naked.

At the sight of him Blythe shook with awe. Lean-muscled, his body was perfect, with square shoulders, well-defined pectorals, flat belly, narrow hips and strong thighs. He was built like a swimmer or a long-distance runner.

"You're so beautiful."

"You're so beautiful."

The pause following was broken by a mixture of startled laughter, a soft feminine moan and an answering male growl before Patrick hauled Blythe down on the bed and covered her body with his own. It wasn't the time for slow exploration, arousing strokes and soft words. They were too far gone with need, too hungry for the other to wait any longer.

Blythe vibrated with the feel of Patrick's heartbeat at her breasts. She savored the husky sounds he made in his throat, felt them mingle with her own as his mouth came down on hers. When his tongue plunged inside, she became a hot, sensual flow of female demand, engulfing him. Her hands closed on his hips, her nails digging into his hard buttocks.

In desperation, Patrick gave way. He could feel her naked breasts swelling against him, her taut nipples stroking him in rhythm with the frantic pulsebeat at her throat. He couldn't breathe until the agonizing tension inside him found release in her softness. Her hips surged upward to meet him, and he plunged forward, with lightning strength and power. "Blythe...Blythe... Blythe!"

"Patrick!" Blythe cried with his entry. She tried to complement the power in him but was overwhelmed by the beauty, overcome by the joy. Spreading, rippling sensation enveloped her, inside and out, all around her, through him. It absorbed everything, became stronger with each deep thrust, every pulsating lunge of his magnificent body. In that radiant, suspended moment before her heart burst, Blythe experienced the ultimate happiness, then lost herself in timeless pleasure.

Patrick felt as if his heart would explode from his chest as shudders ripped through him. He had never felt so complete, so closely joined to another human being. In body and spirit she was woman and he was man, yet they were melded into one. In jubilation he gave her his strength and his passion and something he had never given another. He gave himself.

It was the sweet smell of roses that finally roused Patrick from an insensible stupor. His face was buried between Blythe's lush breasts. Slowly he lifted his head and willed his weak arms and legs to shift off her to the side. She was so still, so quiet that he could barely detect her breathing.

Uncertainly he waited for her to open her eyes. It seemed an eternity before her long sable lashes lifted, and he could gaze into their sapphire blue depths. Searching her expression, he brushed a strand of ebony hair off her forehead, then asked, "Are you okay? I didn't hurt you?"

Hurt? No, she wasn't in pain, at least not any she was conscious of. She felt shattered, but that was because she had yet to recover from a shattering experience. She could see the concern on Patrick's face but couldn't seem to find any words to relieve his anxiety. He was moving, talking, thinking, and she wasn't capable of anything but feeling.

Patrick was no longer inside her, yet she felt as if he were still there. His lips were no longer at her breast, yet her nipples continued throbbing. His hands weren't touching her, yet her skin tingled and burned. Whenever she breathed, she was aware of an aching emptiness that needed refilling, so she tried not to breathe. The harder she tried, the more frightened she became.

Good Lord! What had he done to her? What was she going to do if her body never ceased begging for his? If he somehow sensed how it was for her, she was doomed.

"Blythe! Answer me!" Patrick reached for her shoulder and shook her. "What's wrong!"

The sharp bite of Patrick's fingers accomplished what Blythe's befuddled brain couldn't manage. Within a few seconds, she found her voice and even managed to move slightly away. Her response came out in a slightly hysterical tone, but she couldn't help that. She'd been very close to panic. "Nothing's wrong."

"Thank God," he sighed in relief. "For a minute there, I thought I'd hurt you."

"I'm fine," Blythe lied, drawing the sheet over her breasts as she pushed herself up on the mattress. Pressing her shoulders against the headboard, she tried to think of something clever and sophisticated to say. "I . . . I'm so tired. I can hardly keep my eyes open."

Heaving himself up beside her, Patrick smiled as if she'd just given him a beautiful compliment. "Then sleep, sweetheart. Close your eyes and dream about what we just shared." His tone turned rueful. "I'll stay as long as I can, but then I'll have to go back to my place. I promised Kevin I'd go jogging with him at six tomorrow morning, and I can't very well run in a suit."

Hours later Patrick eased Blythe's head off his shoulder and slid out of her bed. His eyes never left her slender form as he slowly got dressed. Then, after one last lingering look, he trod quietly out of the room. A few moments later he retrieved his suit coat from the living room and left her apartment.

Hours after Patrick's departure, Blythe was still awake.

Six

A buzzing noise, insistent and irritating, assaulted the warm nest of Blythe's slumber. Her eyes still closed, she reached toward her nightstand and smacked the alarm bar on her clock. The buzzing stopped, and in the blessed silence she burrowed her face back into her pillow.

She'd had only a couple of hours of sleep. She must have set the alarm out of habit, but it was Saturday, and there was no need to get up. She could sleep as long as she wanted, put off any more soul-searching for another few hours. After a decent rest, she might be able to make some rational, logical evaluations concerning what had happened to her last night.

The loud buzzing sounded again. Blythe batted at the clock for the second time. Groaning, she fumbled blindly at the alarm, but the buzz continued despite her frantic efforts to turn it off.

Propping herself on her forearms, she squinted at the clock. 7:00 a.m. Her mind still foggy, she considered tossing the infuriating noisemaker across the room. She reached for it but hesitated when the sound stopped, then started again. It was the door buzzer, not the clock, and by the sound of it, whoever was on the other side of the door wasn't going to give up until she answered.

Shoving her fingers through her hair, Blythe let out a disgusted sigh of resignation. Who could be so inhuman as to call on her at this hour? Had they no respect for one of the few days she had off? Furthermore, why had the security guard of her apartment building let someone get this far before notifying her? To get past Fred, her caller had to be someone she knew well.

Becoming more awake, Blythe listed all the possible people who might have the nerve to show up close to the crack of dawn. Her parents? No, they knew their daughter too well. She'd never been a morning person. Even in a crisis, they'd have called first.

Leona? Blythe rejected her secretary, too. She couldn't remember any documents she'd left unsigned or any briefs she needed to go over before Monday. Like Blythe's parents, Leona knew better than to even speak to her boss before she'd had her morning coffee.

That left only one other possibility. Some member of the law force needed her signature on an emergency injunction. Tumbling out of bed, Blythe staggered across her bedroom, shoving her arms into her robe as she went.

The tailored blue velour robe wasn't black judicial garb, but it wasn't a diaphanous peignoir, either. She cinched the belt around her waist as she made her way through her apartment, trying to cloak herself with the dignity of her judicial office as she went. Her hand was on the knob of her front door before she hesitated and peered through the peephole. There was always the chance a stranger might have gotten past security.

The tiny hole provided a wide-sweep, albeit distorted, view of the hallway—and of Patrick. Attired in gray sweatpants and shirt, he stood on the other side of her door, his finger glued to her door buzzer!

His wind-tousled hair, athletic clothing, and the obnoxiously energetic bounce from one foot to the other told her he had met his brother as promised. Joggers, or anyone else who got up with the birds with a smile on their faces and a desire to do any form of exercise, weren't Blythe Cramer's kind of people. She never jogged a step before noon.

Above and beyond her resentment of plucky early birds was the knowledge that she wasn't prepared for another confrontation with this one, not yet. She had lain awake more than half the night trying to figure out what she was going to do about her feelings for Patrick and had found no simple answers. All she knew was that their being involved would bring extremely complex problems to every aspect of her life.

Realizing he wasn't about to go away and give her more time to think, Blythe pasted her most unwelcoming expression on her face and pulled open the door. "Where did you come from?"

Patrick grinned. "About four blocks away. We're practically neighbors, Cramer."

Blythe covered her surprise, thankful he didn't live any closer. "How did you get up here?"

Patrick breezed past her into the apartment, his smile as bright and shiny as a new penny. "Your doorman is a friend of mine," he supplied airily, thinking if he kept her off guard she wouldn't express any of those second thoughts he saw in her beautiful eyes. "Just getting up? You're burning daylight, sweetheart, and it's a beautiful day."

"It's not day yet," she complained irritably. "It's morning. There's a difference. Go away." Blythe stayed at the door, deliberately keeping it open. Placing one hand on her hip, she nodded pointedly at the hallway, hoping he would take himself and all his nauseating vim and vigor right back where he came from. She couldn't talk to him now. She just wasn't up to it.

Patrick stayed where he was in her foyer, grinning as he took in her mussed hair, flushed skin and dew-soft mouth. His grin broadened as his gaze dropped to the ruffled lace at her throat. An expanse of embroidered fragile batiste was exposed by the deep vee opening of her robe. She must have woken up some time after he'd left and slipped into a nightgown. Evidently the lady wasn't comfortable sleeping in the nude.

"Old-fashioned and demure," he teased. "I like that. It makes what's underneath seem all the more alluring."

He took a step toward her, and Blythe took a step backward. "McBride!" she warned firmly as she clutched the edges of her robe together. If he so much as touched her, she'd never be able to convince him that she wanted him to leave.

Though Patrick's smile dimmed a fraction, the glitter in his eyes didn't. He reached around her and closed the door. "You must be one of those people who need a cup of coffee before you can be civil. I can live with that. Point me to your kitchen, and I'll get some started for you."

"What I need is a few more hours in bed."

"An even better idea." Patrick swept an arm around Blythe's waist and hauled her up against him. Wrapping his other arm around her, he bent down and planted a quick kiss on her startled lips. "Good morning, Your Honor," he greeted softly and kissed her again. This time his lips lingered over hers, savored, while his tongue lazily explored and enticed. If he kissed her often enough, reminded her how it was between them, maybe she'd forget all her doubts.

Coherent thought fled as the feel, taste and touch of him reminded Blythe of the wild, wonderful lovemaking they'd shared the evening before. The passionate woman inside her, whom she kept so carefully shrouded in her courtroom, selfishly took over her reason. Patrick was an expert at bringing that woman out. Forgetting why she wanted to keep him at a distance, Blythe melted against him and gloried in the marvelous differences in their anatomies.

Seeking satisfaction for the desire that rippled through her body, she returned his kiss, seeking and enticing as she was being sought and enticed. She slid her palms upward and around his neck. She tugged him downward so that she could deepen the kiss. Snuggling her soft curves against his hard planes, she was gratified to feel him tremble and to hear a low sound in his throat as he gathered her even more tightly against him.

"Another hour or two in bed with you would get the blood moving better than a morning run," he said as he brushed his lips across her cheek and down her throat. He pivoted her around, and while still nuzzling her neck, started shuffling them both toward her bedroom. "Mmmm, you're so warm and cuddly and smell so sweet."

Without his demanding mouth on hers, Blythe was able to summon up some sense. Good God, what was she doing? Was she crazy? This was how she'd gotten herself into this mess in the first place.

Stiffening her spine, she distanced herself mentally from the promise of his body. "You don't smell sweet," she said, trying for a steady voice and a shred of conviction. Patrick smelled of male sweat, but it was an alluring essence mixed with the scent of soap, shaving cream and fresh air.

"I'll take a shower first," Patrick suggested rapidly, not yet aware of her withdrawal. Her pliancy and response to his kisses had been far more than he'd hoped for this morning. He'd feared she'd wake up regretting last night, but she seemed more than willing to be convinced otherwise.

He hadn't arrived with the thought of tumbling her right back into bed, making love to her in a hundred new ways, but he was human. She looked so soft and cuddly, so kissable that he couldn't resist kissing her again. He'd always been one to jump gleefully out of bed in the morning, thinking it a waste to expend any daylight hours in the sack, but for her, he was ready and willing to change his habits.

With the greatest of willpower, Patrick moved his mouth away from hers and slid his lips along the cord of her neck. Another foray into the warm cavern of her mouth, and he'd be pulling her down on the floor and taking her with an urgency he was beginning to think he'd always feel for this woman. For years he'd suspected that there was far more to Blythe Cramer than what appeared on the surface. He'd gotten confirmation of that last night, but each time he was with her brought more revelations.

He raced kisses down her throat while his fingertips traced her spine. Settling his hands over her buttocks, he lifted and pressed her into the cradle of his thighs. She was so soft, so womanly. A man could forget everything when he held her.

Blythe whimpered then shuddered as she felt his desire press against her. Once again they were going too far, too rapidly. Her head was spinning. Her body was responding, clamoring for his without any direction from her mind. All that she was seemed threatened. She had to stop this, couldn't continue responding to him like a mindless puppet on her master's string.

"Patrick..." Her tone wasn't the sharp warning she'd wanted but a soft breathless pronouncement. Her hands dropped limply from his shoulders, and her arms dangled at her sides. She shook her head and cleared it of the sensual haze he'd created. "McBride...stop!" This time she was successful in ridding her voice of sensual entreaty. "I'm not in the mood for this."

He lifted his head and saw the guarded reserve in her eyes, the cool dismissal. *Damn!* So she was still having second thoughts. Major ones from the looks of it. As much as he disliked the idea, he was going to have to give her more time, a little more space.

Carefully and slowly Patrick withdrew from her, his breath coming in jerky gasps. Her unmoved expression made him feel foolish for getting so carried away, but that was just as much her fault as his. He doubted she would agree. He wished that a man had the ability to cover his arousal as easily as a woman could. It gave the fair sex too much of an advantage.

Cloaking himself in a deceptively casual air, Patrick sauntered toward Blythe's kitchen. "What are you serving for breakfast?"

Not sure whether she was grateful or insulted that he'd turned his back on her, Blythe didn't answer immediately. She didn't trust her voice just yet. Her legs were still rubbery, and she very much would have liked to collapse on the nearest chair—that is, if her feet could have carried her that far. Obviously Patrick didn't suffer from the same symptoms. After a kiss that was hot enough to scorch metal, he had nonchalantly shrugged his shoulders and walked away.

Then she heard her refrigerator door open, the clatter of jars and cartons being jostled inside. He was doing it again. Just like last night, he was moving in and taking over, invading her space, challenging her on all levels.

Well, no matter how it seemed to him, she would stand up to the challenge. All through their school and college years, she'd matched him academically, and she could tie or best him on any other level he chose. They'd already learned that she could match him in passion. She could also match his easy withdrawal from it.

"I don't *serve* anyone breakfast, counselor," Blythe informed him coolly as she strode briskly into her kitchen. She hitched herself up on one of the stools at her breakfast bar and rested her tightly clasped hands on the Formica surface.

Patrick closed the refrigerator, crossed his arms and leaned negligently against the porcelain door. The frigid interior of the appliance had helped cool his head, and the rest of his body had followed suit. A drastic measure, to be sure, but blessedly convenient and almost as effective as a cold shower.

As he looked across the room at Blythe, he tightened his lips to keep from grinning. So he wasn't the only one who'd been singed by the heat. Oh, Blythe was good at masking her emotions. Very good. But not quite good enough to convince him that she wasn't still a bit hot.

Her lips were moist, rosy and pouty. She looked like a woman who'd just been thoroughly kissed, and she couldn't hide the signs any more than he could have hidden his arousal. However, he saw more than the evidence of his kisses. There was a touch of huskiness in her tone, and her breathing was rapid. He noted the tiny tremor in her hands as she clasped them tightly together. Even if she was having trouble accepting their intimate relationship, the Honorable Judge Cramer had been highly aroused, and though wild horses wouldn't drag that admission out of her, she hadn't yet recovered.

Could they call this latest match a draw? Or had he managed to beat her in a contest that had started with a good-morning kiss and ended in a battle for dominance? He hoped it was another draw. Sharing passion with Blythe Cramer was a delight. After last night, he'd go fifty-fifty with her anytime.

"Let me rephrase my question, Your Honor," Patrick requested formally. "What were you planning on having for breakfast, and would you be so kind as to share it with this poor, hungry man who found that his cupboard was bare this morning?"

"Couldn't you have jogged on over to the nearest pancake house?" Blythe inquired snidely. Unlocking her fingers, she spread her hands on the top of the counter. The hard surface steadied their shaking.

"Which do you detest more? Breakfast or joggers?" Patrick fired back.

"I'm not sure," Blythe returned honestly. "At the moment, the thought of either turns my stomach."

The last was an out-and-out lie, and Blythe prayed Patrick wouldn't recognize it. The jogger lounging in her kitchen was very appealing. Too appealing. It wasn't fair that he should look so good in a pair of shapeless gray sweatpants and matching shirt—especially at this ungodly hour of the morning.

She frowned at the clock not far above his head. "It's only a little past seven. Have you no decency?"

"Probably not." He pushed himself away from the refrigerator and crossed the short work area. Leaning quickly across the bar, he kissed her forehead. "Since you're not in the mood, you'd better go get dressed before I show you just how indecent I can be. I'll fix breakfast while I'm waiting for you."

"I don't want any breakfast, and I want you out of here."

"You should start the day off right, Blythe," he went on in a paternal tone. "A good breakfast will put roses in your cheeks and a smile on your face," he told her, thinking all the while of a much more pleasurable way to accomplish the same thing.

"I'll have a better breakfast without you."

"You won't eat a thing, and I know it." His tone turned coaxing. "Meals are better if they're shared. That's probably why you don't eat breakfast. You don't like eating alone. It would be to your best interest if I took it upon myself to make sure you always have a morning companion to eat with."

"McBride..."

"Cramer..."

Blue eyes glared into twinkling green ones. Stubborn chins were tilted at the same angle. Two very contrasting bodies were tensed to carry the challenge a step further. And then Patrick laughed. "Go get dressed and wash the night fairy's dust from your eyes. I'm going to win this one, but I won't put it on the tally sheet."

"You're impossibly juvenile." Blythe shook her head, biting her lip to keep from joining in his laughter. How was she ever going to resist this Irish leprechaun whose smile always promised a pot of gold?

"Neither one of us is a juvenile, and if you don't get dressed, I'll prove to you how mature we've become."

Blythe didn't doubt it. She made as graceful an exit as possible under the circumstances. As she hurried toward her bedroom, she vowed that, leprechaun or not, she'd turn around and pound him if he dared laugh at her hasty retreat. He didn't, at least not that she heard.

Breakfast was a simple affair, as Blythe's refrigerator and cupboards were almost as bare as Patrick claimed his to be. Toast and coffee. Saturday was Blythe's grocery shopping day, and also, as she tried to get across to Patrick, she didn't stock typical breakfast foods since coffee was all she required.

"You're going to change your ways," Patrick informed her as he popped the last of his toast in his mouth. "A man could starve to death around here. Things are going to be different now that I'm on the scene."

"McBride, you're not on the scene."

He leaned back in his chair and grinned. The more he thought about it, the better he liked the idea. "Not yet, but I can be all moved in by tonight."

"I'm not even going to dignify that ludicrous suggestion with a response." Blythe gathered her silverware and plate and stood up from the bar. She carried them to the sink. "I'll expect you to clear up your part of this meal as soon as you're finished."

"Is that a house rule?"

"I suppose so," she answered absently as she rinsed her plate.

"Got any others I should know about?" Patrick asked as he came up behind her, dutifully carrying his plate and silverware.

As he reached around her to place his utensils in the sink, he added, "It's only fair that I follow your rules, as it's your apartment."

He propped his hands on the counter, trapping Blythe where she stood. "Now, the way I see it, we can split up the household duties or rotate them, whichever you prefer. I'm not real handy in the kitchen, but you won't starve or be poisoned. I'm pretty accommodating, so it doesn't matter which side of the bed I get. I never leave the shower curtain out, and I hang up my towels. I don't drop my clothes all over the place, and—"

"Hold it right there, McBride." Blythe ducked beneath his arm and put a few feet of safety between them. The warmth of his breath against the back of her neck had been driving her crazy. "I don't need to know how well you've been house-trained."

Undaunted, Patrick went on listing all the traits that he felt qualified him as an acceptable roommate. "I don't squeeze the toothpaste in the middle, and I always put the cap back on. I'll plead guilty to leaving my shoes and socks around, but nobody's perfect. I don't eat crackers in bed, and the only demand I'll put on you is that you do likewise. Cracker crumbs are hellishly scratchy things on naked flesh."

Blythe propped one hand on the counter and tapped her fingernails. "Are you quite finished?"

"Only one more thing. How do I get an assigned parking place in this building?"

"You sign a lease, and they give you one," she supplied through gritted teeth. "Fortunately there are no vacancies. None! Zero! Do you understand my meaning?"

"Sweetheart, you should always wear blue," he returned. His total change of subject completely disarmed her, and Blythe could only gape at him in exasperation. He reached out and lifted her chin with the tip of his finger, effectively closing her mouth.

"Matches those beautiful eyes of yours." His gaze dropped from her face past her tiny waist and trim hips beneath the white poplin shorts. He followed through with a low whistle of appreciation for her tanned, tapered legs. "Great legs, but you ought to roll yourself out and run with me in the morning from now on. It would be a shame to let all you've got get out of shape."

"I prefer to do my exercising at a more decent hour," she maintained. "Like when the sun's on its way *down*."

"Okay, so we'll run in the morning and evening on alternate days. Compromise is expected in every relationship."

He tapped her on the nose, then turned on his heels. As he waltzed through the kitchen door, he announced, "It'll take me a few hours to pack, so I probably won't be back until around six. Don't feel obligated to plan something fancy for dinner. Anything'll do."

Patrick was almost to the front door before the explosion came.

"McBride! You are *not* moving in here! You'll have to look elsewhere for a woman who'll promise not to eat crackers in bed."

Patrick turned around slowly and found Blythe standing with her feet apart, hands on hips, looking for all the world like a sentinel protecting her fortress. He loved the fire of anger flashing in those deep blue eyes of hers every bit as much as he enjoyed the smoky look they took on when she was aroused. With a crooked smile, he asked, "Do you?"

Frowning, she snapped, "Do I what?"

"Eat crackers in bed?"

Blythe squeezed her eyes shut and prayed for deliverance. "It's no concern of yours whether I do or not."

Patrick only smiled condescendingly. For the first time in all their years of competition, Blythe felt she was about to suffer a resounding defeat. She sighed and slumped against the wall. "Patrick, why are you doing this to me? You must realize last night should never have happened," she said in near desperation. "We're like oil and water, an irresistible force and an immovable object. If you and I were the last man and woman on earth, we still wouldn't be right for each other."

"We've always been right for each other," Patrick found himself saying before he had time to think about all the ramifications of such a confession. "We were just too stubborn to admit it. I like almost everything about you, Blythe Cramer. For more than half my life I kept telling myself that you weren't the right woman for me, but last night proved how wrong I was."

His green eyes flaming with longing and passion, he murmured huskily, "I need you, Blythe. We need each other."

"Oh, Patrick." Blythe sighed in despair as she slid down the wall and sat on the floor.

Her legs drawn up, head slumped forward, she stared miserably at her hands dangling between her bent knees.

"Damn your beautiful green Irish eyes," she whispered.

Patrick joined her on the floor. Seated beside her, his position nearly identical to hers, he struggled to keep his hands off her. He wanted to put his arms around her, snuggle close and convince her that all would be well. Together they could handle any obstacles set in their path, but before that could happen, she had to believe it, too. And that would take time. He was willing to bet that, before last night, conservative, cautious Blythe Cramer had never made an impetuous decision in her life.

"You can't move in with me, Patrick. It's too soon for an arrangement like that," Blythe reiterated, breaking the silence. "In another few days we'll probably be at each other's throats and wonder why we thought we could stand each other for more than a minute."

"I know why," Patrick assured suggestively.

"We've got the same academic background and a common interest in law, but that's not much to build on," she insisted, deliberately omitting that other interest they shared.

Patrick wouldn't let her get away with it. "I'd say that's a great foundation, and you purposely left out the best thing. We're wildly attracted to each other, and always have been. Chemistry, for lack of a better way to describe it. But whatever you want to call it, it's there between us, and it's way past time we explored it."

Unable to keep his hands off her any longer, Patrick laid his palm against her cheek. "Darling, nobody has a mouth like yours. I'll never forget the first time I kissed your rosebud lips, and I'm not about to forget all the pleasure they brought me last night." He brushed his mouth across hers, so gently and tenderly that Blythe blinked back tears. He whispered, "I'm not giving up."

"You're not moving in."

"Not today, maybe." He kissed her lightly again. "We'll just spend the evening together. See you around eight."

He leaned toward her, but Blythe pressed her fingers to his lips to prevent them from retaking possession of her mouth. "I have plans tonight."

"Break them," he mumbled against her fingers, then flicked his tongue across them.

Blythe pulled her fingers away, fighting the trembling weakness insinuating itself through her body. "I can't. I mean I won't."

Hauling Blythe onto his lap, Patrick brought his mouth down on hers. He'd prided himself for being a sensitive, skillful lover, but with Blythe, his ability for delicate handling completely deserted him. She was his, dammit! She wasn't going anywhere or doing anything with any man but him.

In an attempt to show her where she belonged, his lips ground harder against hers than he'd intended. He held her much too tightly, as if trying to make her a part of himself. He thrust his tongue into her mouth and branded her with his taste, his passion. And then he deliberately became gentle and played with her tongue, enticing it into his mouth and forcing her to savor as she was being savored.

When Blythe trembled, the arms around her became just as unsteady. When she whimpered, the sound was swallowed by Patrick's mouth. He groaned deep in his throat, and Blythe felt the vibrations in hers. When he tried to lift his head to drag his lips away from hers, thinking that he had proved his point, Blythe's arms came up to pull him back.

Consumed by the need he aroused, she dominated and placed her own brand on him without understanding why she wanted to. Her lips were ardent and seeking, her mouth greedy. Relentlessly she drew him in, her passion equal to his. In this, neither of them could come out ahead or go down in defeat.

Finally, though his heart beat like thunder in his chest, Patrick was able to summon enough strength to drag his lips away from hers. He pressed her head against his chest and held her there while he gulped air and brought his breathing under control.

This woman gave no quarter, and he now knew he was in for the battle of his life. "I was going to say something like 'Remember this while you're out tonight,' but I think touché would be more honest."

Seven

A bright blue sky, decorated with puffs of white clouds, tented the velvety grass and towering trees of River Hill, the Cramer family estate. A gentle breeze blew up from the nearby Scioto River, rustling the leaves of the hardwoods. The low soughing blended with the soft strains of the string quintet playing at one corner of the patio near the house. The breeze wafted through the pines that bordered the edge of the property, picking up their fresh essence and blending it with the scents of roses, geraniums, lavender, thyme and fresh-cut grass. It was summer's delicate perfume, but not one created by nature's whimsy.

Nancy Morris Cramer, the reigning queen of River Hill, had carefully chosen each seedling and directed the planting of each flower bed. The grounds that surrounded the large Tudor-style mansion were perfect. Nancy never settled for less.

The weather this Sunday afternoon was perfect, too. How dare it not be? Blythe mused. The sun always shone on one of her mother's charity fetes.

A series of gaily decorated canopies dotted the grass, lending a festive atmosphere and an illusion of an era long past. The brightly colored canvas didn't shelter knights and their armor, but long linen-draped tables with an array of delicious food. Several smaller tables were provided for the guests' comfort while they ate the sumptuous fare.

The guest list included Columbus's finest and wealthiest, who had each paid a healthy sum for the privilege of partaking of the elaborate "picnic" and eventually having their names engraved on a bronze plaque at the zoo. Few among them would have missed the affair, which was one of the high points in the summer's social calendar. The hostess was not only the granddaughter of a governor, but a descendant of the Morris family that had long shaped the state's political and social history.

No less impressive was the host's lineage. Like the Morrises, the Cramers had also influenced the state's politics and society. Robert Cramer's ancestors had helped carve the state out of the wilderness, and his mother had been the state's first woman judge. His daughter, Blythe, an only child, was following in her illustrious grandmother's footsteps.

So far, having served fifteen months of the three years remaining in her uncle's term at the time of his death, Blythe was proving herself worthy of the judicial legacy handed down to her. Thus far, her rulings had been scrutinized carefully, but declared fair.

Of course, it was expected that Nancy and Robert's daughter would attend the affair, but more than familial duty and an interest in zoo improvements had influenced Blythe's decision to make a generous contribution. The next election was almost two years off, but groundwork had to be laid now. Her name on the list of zoo benefactors wouldn't hurt her civic-minded image.

She had long since learned that politics and garden parties were irrevocably intertwined. For more than two hours Blythe had circulated, smiled, answered questions and listened politely as others expressed their opinions of justice. Her temples were beginning to throb, and her face felt as though it would crack if she had to smile one more time or offer another innocuous reponse.

Though she loved her judicial position, a career she'd dreamed of since she was a little girl visiting her grandmother's office, Blythe didn't particularly enjoy the subtle maneuvering behind the scenes that would help assure her election. She would rather depend totally on her record as a fair and honest judge than on her success in society. But political campaigns needed both monetary and influential backing in order to succeed.

Ideally, the judicial branch of any level of government was supposed to be apolitical. However, that wasn't quite the reality. Once on the bench, a judge didn't consider political ideology in handing down rulings, but during the campaigns to win the seat, party backing was essential. At an affair like today's, the leaders of the Republican party were well represented.

Having decided she'd spent as much time as she could stand socializing and wooing future support, Blythe searched the grounds for her parents. Near the edge of the patio, she saw the dusty rose of her mother's dress amid a cluster of other bright summer dresses and the more somber colors worn by the men.

As Blythe made her way toward the patio, she kept her head tilted downward. The wide brim of her hat hid much of her face, protecting her from the sun and allowing her to slip through the crowd without getting accosted. It also obstructed her line of vision, and she didn't see the man standing off to one side, engaged in an animated conversation with her father.

"Blythe, dear," Nancy Cramer greeted, her sharp gray eyes approving her daughter's tasteful attire. Blythe's tailored blue linen dress, topped with a white cap-sleeved jacket was stylish but appropriately conservative for her image.

Nancy slipped an arm around her daughter's waist. With an inexorable purpose that Blythe couldn't deny, Nancy guided her along toward a couple standing near the sculptured fountain that gurgled pleasantly in the center of the patio. "Look who's here—Warren and Melinda Byers."

Despite her headache, Blythe's smile reflected her genuine joy as she greeted the distinguished silver-haired senator and his wife. "It's wonderful to see you again," she said as she exchanged warm hugs with both of the latecomers. She'd known the couple most of her life and had been involved in several of the senator's reelection campaigns.

Warren Byers held Blythe's hand and smiled warmly down at her. "So pretty little Blythe is now the Honorable Judge Cramer. Your grandmother would have been so proud of you. I represented my first client in her courtroom. I'll never forget it. Florence didn't put up with any shenanigans. I was pretty full of myself, but she made me toe the line. Every attorney in town knew they had to follow courtroom procedure to the letter in Flo's courtroom.''

''Her granddaughter is keeping up that tradition,'' a smooth baritone voice sounded just beyond Blythe's shoulder. ''The present Judge Cramer runs a tight courtroom, too.''

Blythe's heart skipped a beat. All her senses clamored, sending jumbled messages to her brain. Patrick! He was the last person she'd expected to be attending this affair.

A part of her warmed at the sound of his voice, but another part of her started sounding warning bells. Inwardly shrinking, she fortified herself for his next remark. No matter what they'd shared, nor how eloquently he'd denied having any ulterior motives, she didn't quite trust that he wouldn't seize this opportunity to bring up the contempt citation she'd given him—if only to tease her.

Stepping aside and turning slightly, Blythe acknowledged Patrick with a nod of her head, praying that an introduction would stop the bent of the conversation. ''Mr. McBride,'' she greeted politely.

Before she could introduce him to the senator, Warren Byers queried, ''McBride? The Columbus Crusader?''

Patrick extended his hand toward the older man and said a bit sheepishly, ''A reputation hardly deserved, sir, but I am Patrick McBride.''

With the polished demeanor that came from years of political experience, Warren Byers smiled unwaveringly, though Blythe thought she detected an icy glint in his eyes. Right then, she didn't really care how the two men were reacting to each other. She was just grateful that the conversation had been steered away from her and her manner in the courtroom.

Still smiling, Senator Byers remarked, "We've heard of you from as far away as Washington. Got your start in the Public Defender's office, didn't you?"

"My brothers and myself all spent a year working for the county," Patrick said. "We're in private practice now, but I still do *pro bono* work occasionally."

"Commendable," Byers stated dryly. "Even if that's a somewhat idealist approach to take, considering our depressed economy. It takes a large amount of money to keep a private practice going nowadays."

"Winning a case for the little guy is often more gratifying than defending someone who can afford to spend a million on legal fees. The day I consider the fee before taking on a case is the day I'll stop practicing."

"As I said, commendable," Byers reiterated brusquely. "Some are speculating that you may be your party's standard-bearer for my seat some day."

"There's no truth to that rumor, sir," Patrick assured him. "I have absolutely no political aspirations. I'm very content with the work I do and believe that the courtroom is my best arena."

"The courtroom?" the senator asked, still probing. "Are you going after a seat on the bench?"

Patrick shook his head and grinned. Sliding a quick sideways glance at Blythe, he said, "The only aspiration I have in that area is to study the judges themselves in order to know how best to present my case."

Byers chuckled. "So you do your homework and know that you'd better behave like a gentleman in Judge Cramer's courtroom."

Blythe wanted to push Patrick into the fountain's pool and let him swim with the goldfish. That would certainly take the starch out of his crisp navy blazer and white summer pants and dampen his unflagging poise. It would definitely prevent him from responding to the senator's statement.

Unfortunately the drastic measure would draw too much attention, and that was the last thing she wanted. At an affair like this, all areas of the news media were represented, and it would be just her luck to have the whole maneuver taped and shown on the six o'clock news.

Taking a deep breath, she used the only diversionary tactic she could think of. "Senator, I'm afraid I'm going to have to interrupt and steal Mr. McBride away from you." She linked her arm through Patrick's and said, "I promised to introduce him to several people, and since he can't stay much longer, I'd better fulfill those promises before he gets away from us. It was very nice to see both of you again."

With a tug she pulled Patrick away from the senator and his wife, only to run into her mother. "I don't believe we've ever actually met, Mr. McBride," Nancy Cramer commented a trifle icily. "But I've certainly heard a lot about you over the years."

"Mrs. Cramer, it is indeed an honor to meet you. Might I add that you have a lovely home and throw a wonderful party," Patrick said gallantly, turning on the charm that he so easily commanded. "If the attendance here today is any indication, that new primate building at the zoo will be a reality before the year is out. Columbus certainly is lucky to have people like yourself working to make good things happen."

Blythe's mother's cool facade melted a little. Blythe wasn't sure whether it was from the warmth of Patrick's blarney or the heat of her own simmering rage.

Blythe still didn't trust Patrick, and she couldn't figure out how he'd gotten in to the party. The affair was by invitation only, and she was certain his name hadn't been on the guest list.

"Thank you ... Patrick, isn't it?" Nancy asked, oblivious to the discomfort of her daughter. "You were in school with Blythe, I believe."

"Yes, ma'am, we were classmates from first grade through Harvard."

Even Nancy's practiced poise slipped a little, and her eyes reflected her astonishment. She'd had no idea that Patrick had attended Harvard Law School. "I hadn't realized your association with my daughter had continued past high school."

"Our lives have been parallel for years, but now they've finally converged, Mrs. Cramer," Patrick supplied with a devilish grin. "We've...ah...recently met head on, so to speak."

Turning his attention to Blythe, Patrick sent her a sizzling look. His green eyes were verdant as they focused on her lips. Catching the moan that threatened to emerge, Blythe attempted to unlink her arm from Patrick's. No such luck.

As she tugged, he tightened his hold until her arm was locked between his and the solid wall of his chest. For added insurance, he caught her hand and pressed it tightly over his forearm. Smiling, he caressed her wrist with his fingertips. The affectionate gesture was entirely too intimate, making exactly the kind of impression Blythe wished to avoid.

Patrick's touch and closeness were sending tingles over every inch of her body, reminding her all too well of the explosive effect he had on her. Blythe yearned for a glass of something cold to dump on Patrick, or even herself, in order to douse the flames leaping between them.

All the while they waged silent battle, Nancy Cramer kept the conversation rolling. No matter what her opinion was of a guest, she could be counted on to play the gracious hostess. Unlike Blythe, Patrick showed himself to be quite adept at making small talk while speaking another language with his body.

"Oh, you must be referring to the case you tried in front of Blythe this week," Nancy was saying. "Blythe's ruling in your favor warranted a spot on the evening news. It's about time the inconsistencies in our welfare system were brought to light."

"I agree," Patrick returned. "Only time will tell how significant Blythe's ruling will be in determining future cases, but it certainly served one important purpose."

"What's that?" Nancy inquired, always eager to hear favorable remarks about her daughter.

"It brought us together after all these years."

Nancy's polite mask crumpled slightly at the edges, but she managed to say, "I should think you two would have crossed paths in the legal community before this."

"Somehow the fates didn't see fit to be so kind, Mrs. Cramer. That is, not until now."

Blythe had heard enough. Much more of this, and Patrick would be announcing to her mother exactly where he'd spent the better part of Friday night. To add further complication to an already difficult situation, Blythe noticed the society editor for the evening newspaper approaching with a photographer in tow. The last thing she needed was a cozy picture of herself and Patrick splashed all over the newspapers—especially since she'd decided a recent case in Patrick's client's favor. She tried again to extract her arm from his hold, succeeding only because she added a sharp sideways kick to his ankle.

"Mother, I'm afraid we're keeping Mr. McBride," she said, hoping to distract Nancy's attention from the pained surprise on Patrick's face. "He mentioned something about another appointment. Since I have to be leaving now, too, I thought I'd escort him out. It's been a lovely party, as always. Give my love to Dad and tell him I'll—"

"What's this, trying to sneak out without saying goodbye to me?" Robert Cramer interrupted, slipping an arm around his wife as he joined the threesome.

"Ah . . . sorry, Dad. I didn't realize you were anywhere close by." Blythe tried for a genuine smile, though she saw her escape being delayed once again. "Dad, may I introduce—"

"Patrick and I have already met," her father finished for her. "It was a pleasure, I might add."

"All mine, sir," Patrick returned sincerely.

The newswoman was getting closer, but the photographer had stopped to take several pictures of Senator Byers. Blythe couldn't afford any time for idle chit-chat. Stepping forward, she gave both her parents perfunctory kisses on the cheek and started edging away. "I know you'll excuse us. We really have to be going." She turned on her heels and prayed Patrick would follow.

Choosing the quickest path to safety, Blythe headed for the open French doors at the edge of the patio. She looked over her shoulder for Patrick as she stepped into the house and breathed a sigh of relief that he was right behind her. Not looking where she was going, she took another step into the house and collided with a human wall. Recoiling too quickly, she fell back against Patrick who caught her around the waist.

Blythe's hat slipped forward as she strove to maintain her balance. "I'm so sorry," she apologized as she swept the bothersome hat from her head and addressed the man she'd bumped into.

When she recognized him, she wished she'd left the confection of bleached straw and ribbons in front of her face. Standing before her was local newspaperman Bob Whittiker. The man was notorious for exposing scandals in his weekly column. Though most people knew Whittiker's stories were rarely documented, his sly comments still planted the seeds of doubt and speculation.

"The Honorable Judge Cramer! And the Columbus Crusader! Together? How interesting. Didn't I see you two chatting with our host and hostess just now? Was that a cozy little family gathering by chance? Possibly portending things to come? They do say opposites attract, don't they?"

Whittiker asked his questions loudly, with the obvious intent of attracting attention. Fortunately for Blythe and Patrick, there was no one else close by. He paused between each of his questions only long enough to register the expressions on his victims' faces. Blythe tried to keep her features bland, but with his last question, couched in snide innuendo, he drew a gasp of shock from her. "Or is this a case of politics making for strange bedfellows?"

Patrick smoothly inserted himself between Whittiker and Blythe. "Whittiker, you're drilling in a dry hole. If you'd done your homework, you'd know that Judge Cramer and I are long-time acquaintances. What you see is nothing more than two old friends sharing a pleasant afternoon and reminiscing about our school days. If you're smart, you'll get on out there with the rest of your colleagues, clustered around Senator Byers, and go for some real news. I've heard that he's about to make some sort of announcement. I believe he was saying something about the president.''

"Byers is here?" Whittiker asked, his face flushed with excitement. "The president, you say." The man pushed past Blythe and Patrick in a rush.

Blythe waited until Whittiker was well out of earshot. "The president?" She raised a brow, pushing her tongue in her cheek to keep from laughing.

"Yes, Byers was looking for the president of the zoo docents. Seems he was going to make some announcement about the newly elected officers of the board."

"Whittiker is going to go after your scalp when he finds out how you tricked him," Blythe warned with a giggle of pure enjoyment at the way Patrick had handled the irksome reporter.

"Probably," Patrick agreed. "But, with any luck, he'll notice that a...uh...special friend of the senator's is out there, too. Maybe Whittaker will go after that story and leave us alone."

"Oh, no," Blythe cried in dismay. "Melinda Byers doesn't deserve that kind of gossip being printed."

"She's weathered it before," Patrick informed her dispassionately as he caught Blythe's arm and steered her farther into the house. "Nice, very nice." He stopped and looked around the stately living room, making a quick survey of the gracious and rich furnishings. "How about giving me a tour? I've always been curious about the castle where Princess Blythe grew up."

"A tour of the house?" Blythe asked as she moved away from Patrick. She was grateful to see that the room was totally empty. "McBride, we've just escaped from what could have been a very sticky situation. I'm leaving right now, and I'd suggest you do the same."

She had crossed to the middle of the large Aubusson carpet that centered one of the conversation groupings scattered about the room. Stopping abruptly, she whirled around. "How did you get in here in the first place?"

"Walked right in the front door, like everybody else." He grinned down at her with that leprechaun grin that always made her uneasy. His eyes full of emerald mischief, he declared, "I've been a zoo patron for a long time. I like animals, especially monkeys."

"I can certainly understand that," Blythe returned dryly. "I don't think you're that far removed."

"Hey, I left all those bananas alone out there."

"Good for you," Blythe commented and tried for an escape again. "See you sometime, McBride."

Patrick caught up with her as she passed through the living room doorway and into the large formal foyer. "Sometime?" he demanded as he spun her around to face him. "Cramer, sometime is from now on. Like I told your mother, our paths have finally converged. In case you haven't guessed it yet, they're staying converged. I'm not letting you slip away from me for another eighteen years."

The mischief was gone from Patrick's eyes, and in its place was dark intent. Blythe stared up into his face, seeing the implacable set of his jaw, the firm line of his mouth and the absence of any sign of humor. He was dead serious, and she knew that Friday night had meant more to him than a one-night stand. The worry that she had become the latest in the string of McBride women faded a little more. At the same time the realization strengthened that she very much wanted to mean a great deal to Patrick McBride.

"Keep looking at me like that, and I'm going to kiss you right here," Patrick threatened softly, his features relaxing and his eyes lambent with desire. "That mouth of yours is like a magnet for mine. I want to hold you, kiss you, taste you and feel you pressed against me."

"Patrick! Hush! Anyone could walk in right now." Blythe looked around, certain that if anyone should happen to wander by they'd know exactly what he'd just said to her. They might not have overheard him, but she was sure the flush she felt in her cheeks would broadcast her response. He was dangling in front of her all the temptations she was trying so hard to overcome.

Patrick looked around the vacant foyer, seeing only the polished wooden floor, the expensive Oriental runner and the priceless antique furnishings. "Nobody around, so let's dash upstairs. I want to see the room where you slept when you were little and then later when you were the sexiest girl I ever knew."

Not waiting for an answer, he caught her hand and started up the wide staircase. She followed along in his wake, sure that if she tried to stop he'd just drag her along or pick her up and carry her.

Showing him her old bedroom seemed totally ridiculous. Being in any bedroom with Patrick was dangerous, but in the past three days she'd come to recognize more than a few things about him. When he was really intent on doing something, nothing short of a major scene would prevent him from carrying it through.

Anyone who was anyone in the city was gathered in her parents' backyard, and most of the news media were out there, as well. This wasn't the time for a scene. That was exactly what she'd been trying to avoid for the past half hour or more. "McBride, why are you doing this?" she demanded as she tried to keep up with him.

Patrick didn't break his rhythm as they conquered the first flight, turned on the landing and started up the last few steps. "Ah, we're back to putting a little distance between us again, are we? You only call me Patrick when I've really gotten to you or we're making love. Afraid I'll pull you into one of these rooms, lock the door and ravage you for the next hour or so?"

Sure that she heard voices coming closer, Blythe pulled Patrick through the closest bedroom doorway. She closed the door quickly behind them, slipping the lock for insurance. Leaning back against the paneled door, she clutched her hat and purse defensively to her breasts. Breathing heavily, she closed her eyes and shook her head. "Patrick," she whispered. "You are... are..."

"The man who's dying to kiss you. It's been over twenty-four hours, and I'm starving."

Blythe was pulled into his arms, and his lips covered hers before she could open her eyes. She didn't open them, but succumbed to the magic of his kiss, shutting out everything but Patrick, his touch, scent and taste. His mouth moved possessively over hers as his arms tightened around her shoulders and waist, then abruptly dropped.

"These are definitely in the way," he said against her lips as he pulled her crushed hat and purse from between them and tossed them aside. "I want to feel you, not your hat."

His arms slipped under her jacket, and his hands spread wide over her back and buttocks. He pressed her into the solid strength of his body as he fused their mouths again. Blythe's arms and hands followed Patrick's example. Bypassing the barrier of his linen blazer, she splayed her fingers wide over his back, reveling in the feel of hard muscle, separated from her touch by one thin layer of fine cotton.

Being held by Patrick, sharing a kiss with him, was magic. Blythe felt as if she were floating, then spinning, into a world of beautiful colors. It was a special place of exquisite sensations, so powerful that they camouflaged everything else until there was nothing but Patrick.

"Man oh man, kissing you is a real mindblower," Patrick said shakily. He loosened his hold on her and linked his hands at the small of her back. Taking several deep breaths, he brought his heartbeat closer to normal.

Blythe put a little space between herself and Patrick but kept her palms against his chest for support. "What brilliant oratory, counselor."

"Kiss me again, Your Honor, and I'll qualify for living space in that planned new facility at the zoo."

"Maybe I should," she teased coyly. "Climbing out on limbs seems to be your specialty."

Patrick looked puzzled, and Blythe supplied an explanation as she stepped out of his arms. "Now that we're up here, how do you suggest we get back downstairs and out of this house without anyone guessing where we've been and what we've been doing?" She could still taste Patrick on her lips, and her body was still warm and tingling with arousal, but the jeopardy they were in forced her mind to concentrate on other things beyond the pleasure of being in his arms.

"First, you march over to that mirror and do the best you can to restore your makeup," he suggested, grinning as she rushed to the mirror to appraise the damage. While Blythe retrieved her purse, rummaged through the contents for repair supplies, Patrick sauntered around the room. "This is it, isn't it?"

"What?" Blythe fluffed her hair with a small brush.

"Your old room." He fingered the ruffled curtains at the window, smiled at the dainty flowered wallpaper and ran his hand over the eyelet bedspread on the canopied bed. "You like beds with roofs, don't you?"

"I hadn't thought about it quite like that, but I guess I do."

He studied the momentos arranged in a glass-fronted cabinet hung on the wall over an Empire-style desk. "Interesting," he commented vaguely as he moved his attention to the arrangement of framed photographs and certificates above a bookcase. "We can go now, if you've got yourself together. I found out what I wanted to know."

"And exactly what was that?" Blythe asked in a whisper as she leaned her ear toward the closed door.

"You're a collector, a saver, and your family and the past mean a lot to you."

"So?"

"Just wanted to make sure."

"McBride, you're crazy."

"Yeah, probably. Got a back stairs we can sneak down?"

There was, and, like two thieves, Patrick and Blythe made their way down the narrow winding stairway that ended inside a small wood-paneled room. "I thought that was the servants' staircase and we'd end up in the kitchen," Patrick remarked.

"This was my grandmother's study. She had the house built this way so she could go from here to her bedroom without going through the whole house," Blythe explained, keeping her voice very soft as she carefully cracked open the door leading into the hallway.

"That's your grandmother, the Honorable Judge Florence Cramer," Patrick stated as he studied the oil painting hanging above the small brick fireplace on one wall.

A dark-haired woman, robed in black judicial garb, looked down at him. Her expression was serious, but the artist had created a delightful sparkle in her deep blue eyes. There was also a hint of a dimple in each cheek. The artist had done a remarkable job of portraying a woman of intelligence, purpose and life. "She must have been quite a woman."

"Yes, she was. Come on, the coast is clear."

"You look a lot like her. Must be why they named you Blythe Florence. Did your parents plan from the cradle for you to be a judge?"

"Quit questioning my parents' motives, and let's get going!"

"Yes, Your Honor."

Patrick followed Blythe's lead, and a short time later they passed through the front of the house and out the front door. Luck had turned in Blythe's favor, for the only people they saw were one of the uniformed maids, supplied by the catering service, and the teenage boy hired to park cars.

When Blythe's silver Audi sedan arrived, Patrick quickly opened the passenger door and with a gentle push of his hand started to guide Blythe inside. "I'll drive."

"But what about your car?"

"I came with a friend, and he's already left. I told him I'd find a ride. I was pretty sure you wouldn't mind seeing me home." He pushed her down on the plush bucket seat and closed the door on her sputtering protest.

As soon as he'd seated himself behind the wheel, Blythe stated angrily, "This really does it! What if someone sees us leaving together?"

Patrick put the car in motion and started down the long driveway. "What's the matter? You still afraid to be seen with that wild McBride kid?"

Eight

Blythe let Patrick's question drop into silence, unwilling to acknowledge the truth. As a teenager, being seen with him would have ruined her reputation, and nothing had changed. He was the flamboyant Columbus Crusader, an idealist and a liberal. She was a sober, conservative judge and a realist—the reality being that having an affair with him might adversely affect her career.

In the political arena, there were strict rules to be followed and appearances were often more important than fact. As a judge, especially a female judge, she was expected to walk the straight and narrow. Unlike Patrick, she avoided taking risks. If her reluctance to thumb her nose at convention made her a snob in his eyes, then she supposed she was stuck with the label.

They were several miles down the road before she spoke again. "Where are we going?" she demanded

suspiciously as Patrick turned off the road leading back
to the near-north side and onto a residential side street.

"We spent all afternoon with your folks, so I thought
my family deserved equal time," Patrick announced
glibly. "Isn't that the traditional way of doing things?
Boy meets girl's parents, then if all goes well, boy brings
girl home to mother."

"Home to mother!" Blythe was appalled. This situation with Patrick was rapidly getting out of hand. After one weekend he was making all sorts of as-
sumptions, and the more she pulled back, the more he
pushed. She wasn't prepared to meet his parents, and
certainly not ready to give such a serious connotation to
the meeting. What could he be thinking of?

She stared at him, annoyed and confused, until she
noted the devilish spark in his eyes. "Since when have
you ever done anything the traditional way? Why are we
really going to see your parents?"

"To be honest," Patrick began, though when he'd
seen her expression, he'd decided to lie. "We're stopping in because it's getting close to dinnertime. If we
play our cards right, neither one of us will have to do
any cooking today."

Blythe exclaimed in exasperation, "We can't just
drop in unannounced and expect your family to serve
us dinner!"

"Unannounced is the best way with my family,"
Patrick asserted, this time more truthfully. "The less
time my mother has to prepare herself for meeting the
woman in my life, the better."

"I'm not the woman in your life," Blythe insisted
stubbornly, as she'd been attempting to do all day.
Then, as she considered what else he'd said, she unwit-
tingly acknowledged that position by demanding fur-

ther clarification. "What do you mean, the less time she has to prepare for me, the better?"

"You'll know what I mean as soon as you meet her," Patrick evaded, wincing at her dark glare.

"I met her once in the third grade, but I'm not meeting her again until you tell me," Blythe declared shortly.

Squirming beneath her pointed look, Patrick admitted, "Well...eh...my mother's sort of got this thing about grandchildren."

"She's got this thing about grandchildren," Blythe repeated, rolling her eyes.

"She wants lots of them, and so far she's only got one. Sean got married a few years back and came through with a son last year, but the rest of us are still on the hook."

Blythe swallowed hard, then found her voice. "Are you saying your mother views any woman you bring home as the possible mother of future McBrides?"

"I'm afraid so."

"I see," Blythe choked out.

"Would that be so bad?" Patrick inquired wistfully.

Blythe had a hard time not responding to the endearing expression on his face or the sensual entreaty in his eyes. At his question, she pictured herself as his wife, imagined the child they might make together. A sturdy redheaded boy with dimples and his mother's blue eyes. Or perhaps a dainty little girl with a head of shiny black curls and her father's green eyes.

No, it wouldn't be so bad being mother to Patrick's children. It would be wonderful. What was she thinking?

Blythe forced the picture from her mind. Whatever came of her involvement with Patrick, marriage and children had no place in her life for some time yet. She had so much left to accomplish in her career. There was so much she had yet to do before she considered taking such an important step, if she ever did. She was past thirty already. Her childbearing years would soon be over. She couldn't afford to dwell on the lovely but slim possibility that she might one day get married and start a family.

However, since Patrick had just made sure all she could think about was being married to him and bearing his children, she needed some way to avoid making a direct answer to his question. He would sense the deep yearning she felt if she gave a completely honest answer, and Patrick was adept at using her innermost feelings against her. She had to keep reminding herself that she was dealing with a man whose line of blarney was a mile long. To persuade her back into his bed, he kept tantalizing her with evocative sensual pictures.

Thinking frantically, Blythe recalled a tidbit of information she'd heard from a friend back in their school days. "Your mother won't see me that way," she assured Patrick in her most condescending tone.

Patrick was surprised by her confidence and irked by her tone. He wondered what gave her the idea that Molly McBride wouldn't consider her a viable candidate for the role of his wife. Was it so impossible for Blythe to imagine herself, an elite Cramer, as the mother of his children?

"Why not?" Patrick bit out, swerving the wheel as he turned sharply onto a narrow concrete drive.

With her shoulder pressed against the door, Blythe got a passing glance at a white two-story house before they sped up the drive. Her eyes were squeezed tightly shut by the time Patrick brought the car to a jolting stop less than a foot behind one of several parked cars—a flashy red Porsche.

Opening one eye, Blythe released her pent-up breath and muttered in relief, "That was too close for comfort. Drive much, McBride?"

Without sparing a glance for the expensive car he'd so narrowly missed, Patrick faced Blythe and repeated, "Well, why wouldn't my mother consider you a possible candidate for the role?"

Blythe wrinkled her nose at him and sniffed haughtily, "It should be perfectly obvious."

"Not to me," he snapped furiously. "Evidently we lesser mortals don't see things as clearly as you higher beings."

"Evidently not," Blythe agreed loftily. Then, fearing that the throbbing blood vessel at his temple might break, she asked, "Really McBride! How could you think that your dear mother would want 'old snoot face' here to provide her with grandchildren?"

Patrick blinked, shook his head and blinked again, momentarily speechless.

Blythe tried, but the look on his face was so comical that she couldn't control herself. The trapped amusement broke free. Her blue eyes dancing, she burst out laughing. "Gotcha!"

"How did you find out I...? Who told you that's...?" Patrick stumbled and stammered, but then his sense of humor took over, and his laughter joined hers. "You little sadist! You enjoyed doing that to me, didn't you?"

"Immensely, McBride," Blythe admitted between giggles. "Immensely."

"Little brother, if you're laughing at how close you came to ramming into my gorgeous car, I fail to see the joke," a low voice barked outside Patrick's window.

It took Patrick a few seconds to respond. "Sorry, Neal. I was just showing off for the lady."

Blythe would have recognized Neal McBride from the pictures she'd seen of him in the paper if he'd stood still long enough for her to get a look at him, but he didn't. In the blink of an eye he had rounded the Audi and pulled open her door. With the flamboyant gallantry she suspected was bred into all McBride men, he leaned down and offered her his hand. "May a man less juvenile than his brother assist you from the car, Judge Cramer?"

Blythe couldn't help but smile back at a man whose dimples had dimples. Neal sported a pair of green eyes so similar to Patrick's that Blythe couldn't resist them. She didn't stop to question his easy identification of her, assuming he'd recognized her the same way she had him.

She tossed her crumpled hat into the back seat, then gave Neal her hand. "You certainly may."

She was slightly unnerved by the triumphant grin Neal cast Patrick as he helped her from the car and felt even more nervous when she saw two more men who were cut from the same colorful Irish cloth sauntering down the drive. Was male swagger an inherited trait? she wondered in bemusement as she watched their approach.

"The invasion has started," Patrick grumbled under his breath as he came to Blythe's side and quickly commandeered her from his older brother. "What are all you guys doing here, anyway?"

"I don't know about these two," Sean spoke first. "But I can only eat so much bouillabaisse. Carla made enough to feed an army."

An inside joke, Blythe decided, as all three men groaned in sympathy with their oldest brother. Seeing the confusion on her face, Sean apologized, "If you'd ever tasted my wife's cooking, you'd understand what I mean, Your Honor."

He shot a fearful glance at the house. "Carla's a wonderful woman, and I love her dearly, but her culinary skills leave something to be desired. Mom always grills steaks Sunday night. I convinced Carla we need a change of pace, but if she ever finds out I detest her bouillabaisse, I'm a dead man."

"Your secret's safe with me," Blythe said. "And please call me Blythe."

Sean confiscated Blythe's arm and started walking up the sidewalk toward the front door. "I'm glad Patrick brought you along. I've been hoping for a chance to congratulate you. I've been trying to convince Patrick he can't get so carried away in the courtroom, but a nice little contempt charge said it so much better than I ever could."

Blythe felt the color come up on her cheeks as she tossed a questioning look at Patrick. How much had he told his family? Everything, she decided when she noted the brick-red shade of his complexion. Evidently he'd already taken a great deal of ribbing on the subject. After meeting this group, she could just imagine what they'd put him through.

For some reason, Blythe found herself speaking in Patrick's defense. "It was an extremely emotional case. I'd probably have reacted just as strongly as Patrick if I'd been in his shoes. Three children were about to be unfairly taken from their mother's custody, and because of your brother's defense, the woman now has the means to keep her family together.''

"Yeah!" Patrick exclaimed, his expression showing both surprise and gratitude. "Winning the case was well worth the fifty-dollar fine I had to pay for my understandably zealous approach."

"I can't wait to read the transcript," Kevin interjected smoothly as he completed the same maneuver recently employed by his older brothers. Within seconds Blythe was walking in step with the youngest McBride, and Sean, Neal and Patrick were taking up the rear. "Since no one else has seen fit to introduce us, I've been forced to take it upon myself. I'm Kevin, the youngest, most mannerly and best-looking member of the family."

"So I see," Blythe replied, trying hard to keep pace with the exuberant foursome who swept her along in their midst. As they proceeded up the front steps and into the house, she wasn't allowed time to worry about meeting their parents or the possible significance Patrick had placed on the event.

Blythe gained an impression of comfort and warmth as she was escorted through a living room and large kitchen. She had little chance to make polite comment as she was quickly hustled through a pair of sliding glass doors and out into the McBrides' spacious backyard. As soon as they were outside, she and Patrick were deserted by the brothers, who decided to play a game of badminton before dinner. Even so, Blythe was only given enough time to take passing note of a wide brick patio, a well-kept lawn and a lovely rose arbor before Patrick was introducing her to his father.

"So this is Blythe Cramer." Thomas McBride handed a pair of tongs to a big, bearish-looking man as he stepped away from the gas grill situated at one side of the patio. After wiping his hands on his red chef's apron, he grasped hold of Blythe's fingers and began pumping her arm. "I'm glad to shake hands with the one woman who could always give my boyo a run for his money. Now that I see you, I remember you well."

Although Blythe didn't share the memory, she offered politely, "It's nice to see you again, too, Mr. McBride."

"You were a pretty little lady even back then, but just look at you now. 'Course it takes brains, not looks, to get on the bench," Thomas complimented. Drawing her slightly away from Patrick, he went on jovially, "Sharing honors with you in school used to give our Paddy fits. Thought he'd choke the day he found out you passed the bar with the same score."

The glance Blythe gave Patrick told him how much she wished he had choked, but the smile she offered his father was enchanting. "I didn't realize we shared honors there, too," she lied, wondering if Patrick had bribed the same person she had to obtain the information. "But then, *Paddy* and I rarely compared notes in those days."

Patrick tried not to scowl at her lethal expression and forced himself not to blink an eye at her mocking use of his nickname. He stifled a groan as his father continued pounding nails into his coffin. "When Paddy called this afternoon to tell us he was bringing you along to dinner, we couldn't have been more surprised. I've watched him run in the opposite direction just at the mention of your name."

"Oh? Why was that?" Blythe inquired sweetly. Her blue eyes told Patrick he should have kept on running while he had the chance.

"This is Nolan Rooney," Patrick broke in before his father could respond to Blythe's query. "My god-father, family friend and cook *extraordinaire*."

Blythe couldn't help but like Nolan. His smile was wide and welcoming, his gaze admiring and his manner shy. He was a giant of a man, yet blushed like a young boy when she shook hands with him. "Glad to meet you, Mr. Rooney."

Nolan dropped her hand as soon as he could, but he wasn't trying to be rude. To Blythe's delight, he clapped Patrick on the back so forcefully that he almost fell over. "About time you developed some taste, Paddy boy. This is one classy lady. Not your usual... oops... steaks are calling."

"Thank you," Blythe said, uncertain whether she or Patrick was more thankful that Nolan hadn't completed his sentence.

"Judge Cramer," a soft lilting voice sounded behind Blythe. "Welcome to our home. I'm glad you were able to accept Patrick's invitation."

Blythe turned around, sensing a reticence in this greeting that had been lacking in the others. "I'm pleased to be here, Mrs. McBride," Blythe replied, feeling somewhat like a bug on a pin as her features were dissected by a beautiful pair of all-seeing green eyes. "Thank you for having me. I'm sorry this was arranged on such short notice."

Molly McBride didn't look pleased by the apology. "Patrick's friends are welcome here anytime, even without an invitation. We grill steaks most Sundays, so it was no trouble to pull one more from the freezer."

Blythe was disconcerted by the frosty nip in the pleasant words. "I hope not," she replied uneasily, her eyes seeking Patrick's.

"Ma, Blythe had nothing to do with my not being invited to that affair at her folks' home," Patrick put in quickly. "It was a charity thing, and the guest list was decided months ago."

"I'm sure it was," Molly agreed smoothly, then turned to the picnic table located in the middle of the yard beneath a large shade tree. "Patrick, why don't you go introduce Judge Cramer to Carla."

"Please call me Blythe, Mrs. McBride," Blythe requested, hoping to reduce the formality between them.

"Of course," Molly replied, though she didn't call Blythe by name. Smiling warmly at the two women seated at the table, she went on proudly, "Carla is Sean's wife and the mother of our first grandchild, Ryan Thomas. That lovely girl sitting next to her is Tamarra Wilson. She and Neal announced their engagement last night. Now if you'll excuse me, I have to go inside and check on the potatoes."

Patrick frowned after his mother's retreating form, then felt a pair of eyes burning into his face. "You'll have to forgive her, Blythe. I was here using the phone this morning. I should have known her nose would get out of joint when she heard me finagling my way into your parents' party."

"How did you finagle your way in?" Blythe asked, not out of disapproval but curiosity. It wouldn't be fair of her to be angry with his mother; her own hadn't exactly rolled out the red carpet for Patrick.

"We Democrats have a few connections in high places, too," he retorted grandly. "I'm owed some political favors. Charlie Otis is not only on city council, but on the zoo board. It so happens he has an office next to ours. Don't let this get out because it might ruin him politically, but he's up to his ears in debt to McBride and McBride. In the past year alone, he's stolen gallons of coffee off us, not to mention the doughnuts. I threatened to cut off his source of caffeine and chocolate, and *voilà*, he offered to get me in."

"And your mother didn't approve?"

Patrick's smile was slightly sheepish. "She didn't approve of the begging and groveling I went through before making the threat. I guess she thought I should have had more pride." He gave Blythe an affectionate tap on the nose. "But we know that where you're concerned, I have no pride. To get close to you, I'll do more than grovel."

"You'll have to do more, McBride." Blythe amazed herself with the deliberately provocative retort. "A lot more."

"Because I'm up against some strong competition?" Patrick's eyes flashed with anger as he posed the question that he'd tried his level best not to ask her all day. In self-disgust he acknowledged that what he'd just told her in jest was painfully true. Where she was concerned, he did have no pride. "Who were you out with last night?"

Taken aback by the unexpected switch in subject, Blythe realized—and not for the first time—that Patrick could never be counted upon to behave logically. To hold her own with him, she always had to be on the lookout for the next curve he might throw her way. Beyond that, she never knew when he was being serious or when he was kidding. She disliked his knack for keeping her off-balance, and her displeasure showed. "What gives you the right to ask?"

Patrick moved closer so that she could feel the warmth of his body. His eyes trapped hers before moving to her mouth. "That's a good question, Blythe. I was hoping you knew the answer."

"Maybe I don't want to answer," she murmured shakily, revealing that she was afraid of what might happen if she did. If she confessed that her feelings for him gave him the right to ask anything of her, she'd be handing over a weapon that she couldn't trust him not to use. No matter what he said, she couldn't see him committing to anything more than a lusty, torrid affair. Judges didn't have lusty, torrid affairs. "Maybe I can't afford to."

Patrick reached for her hand, tucked it under his arm and began walking toward the picnic table. "You can, and sooner or later you will. In the meantime we'd better go do what my mother said."

After very short acquaintance, Blythe decided she was going to like both Carla McBride and Tamarra Wilson. Carla was a brunette with laughing brown eyes and a dry wit. Tamarra was a statuesque blonde whose guileless blue eyes and baby-doll features hid a rapier-sharp mind. Within minutes Blythe saw how they were able to attract the eldest two McBride brothers and knew why the attraction had developed into something more meaningful. Once introductions were made, Patrick was sent off to "play" with his brothers.

"Whew!" Tamarra bestowed a grateful smile on Blythe as soon as Patrick left them. "Glad you came, Blythe. It takes some of the pressure off me. Neal warned me, but I still wasn't prepared for the inquisition. When you showed up, we were really getting down to the nitty-gritty, like exactly how long I planned to wait before opting for motherhood.''

Carla laughed. "Until after the wedding would be nice, but Molly wouldn't be that upset if you produced an infant right after the reception.''

"You're kidding!" Blythe and Tamarra exclaimed at the same time.

Carla reached into a nearby cooler and passed them each a can of soda. She opened a can for herself and took a long drink before saying, "All it takes to get on Molly's good side is a promise that you won't let the McBride line die out. I've already done my part. I'm just grateful she doesn't expect me to produce four boys like she did.''

Tamarra gazed across the yard where the four males in question were making badminton look like a grudge match to the death. "You should be. Just look at them. They act like they're going to kill one another. How do you suppose she put up with them when they were little?''

"Molly might be a small woman, but I heard she carried a mighty big stick," Carla said. "Whenever Sean gets too far out of line, I open my middle desk door, and he backs down right away.''

"Why's that?" Blythe asked.

"That's where we keep the ruler.''

Patrick didn't like the uproarious female laughter that drifted across the backyard to the playing field. Kevin didn't seem to notice. Sean didn't appear to mind. Neal looked anxious.

Since Neal was his badminton partner, Patrick thought he might have a good chance to convince him they should throw the game and get back to their women. It would be just like Carla to drag some skeletons out of the family closet. There were a few stories he'd just as soon Blythe didn't hear.

Neal felt the same way about Tamarra. Working together, Neal and Patrick were able to lose the next two points with a minimum of bad acting, but since neither of them complained at their defeat, Kevin and Sean saw through their ploy. When it was time to drink to their victory, the winners found themselves alone at the beer keg. "What do you think, Sean?" Kevin inquired before downing his first swallow. "Who's got the biggest ring through his nose, Neal or Patrick?"

Sean finished off half his cup, intercepted a speaking glance from his wife, then lifted a hand to his nostrils. "I do, little brother. No doubt about it," he complained good-naturedly as he set off across the lawn.

If Blythe lived to be a hundred, she didn't think she'd ever forget her first meal with the McBrides. Her mother was considered an organized woman, but Nancy Cramer was a novice compared to Molly McBride. Contained within a slight five feet tall female body was a strict military commander. Molly called her troops and supervised from the kitchen window.

As Blythe watched the McBride brothers get up from the table and meekly go do their mother's bidding, her astonishment must have been clear, for Carla patted her hand and grinned. "Get them when they're young, and you can train them right. I'm considering sending Ryan to live with Sean's mother for the first few years. When he gets back, I'll be able to sit back and take it easy."

"They do this all the time?"

"Theirs is but to serve," Carla confided facetiously, chuckling when she saw the awestruck look on Tamarra's face as Neal placed a platter of steak in front of her, then politely asked what she wanted to drink with her meal. Patrick and Sean repeated the process for Blythe and Carla, then went back into the house to fetch their drinks.

"No matter what anyone else thinks about her," Carla enthused, "I absolutely adore my mother-in-law. I haven't done dishes once since I joined the family. Not only that, but Sean does laundry, vacuums the rugs and makes the bed as often as I do."

"I'm eloping tonight," Tamarra decided before the others joined them at the table. "Right after I tell Molly that I simply adore the thought of having babies."

"If Neal's anything like Sean," Carla supplied knowingly, "you'll adore more than that."

Blythe glanced at the twinkling diamond on Tamarra's finger and felt a funny lurching sensation in her stomach. As far as she could tell, the McBride brothers were a lot alike. When Patrick slid in next to her at the table, it took a great deal of willpower not to place a possessive hand on his warm, hard thigh.

"Hope you like what we're serving tonight, ladies," Sean said as he placed a large bowl of salad in the center of the checkered tablecloth and took his place next to Carla.

The three young women at the table exchanged glances, then met the sparkling green eyes of their hostess. "I'm sure we will, darling," Carla confirmed the feelings of the others. "What's not to like?"

Nine

I liked your family. Every one of them," Blythe said, smiling at Patrick as he backed out of the McBride driveway. "And I thought your mother warmed up considerably by the end of the evening. Didn't you?"

"Uh-huh," Patrick muttered, barely paying attention to her as he thought about an earlier conversation they'd had with his mother. If Blythe liked his family so much and understood that the feeling was mutual, why hadn't she wanted to join them at the Stag's Head tomorrow evening? Was an off-campus bar too lowly for the princess of River Hill? Too undignified for the Honorable Judge Cramer?

Blythe studied the grim expression on his face. "Is something the matter?"

Patrick gave her a blank look, then shook his head as if to clear it. "We've got a big problem, Cramer."

"We do?"

Patrick nodded. "My family liked you," he confirmed. They sure as hell had. So much so, he had almost seen the cogs turning inside his mother's head as she saw another son settled. Now Molly McBride could direct all her efforts toward the last remaining bachelor since she had Blythe and him practically walking down the aisle. But did Blythe have that in mind? No!

"That's a problem?" Blythe asked after a disconcerting pause.

If she had thought she was confused earlier, now she was sure of it. Hadn't the purpose of their visit to his parents been to introduce her in the hope that they'd like her and she'd like them? As always, just when she thought she had Patrick figured out, he switched tracks altogether. Maybe for some strange reason he hadn't wanted his family to like her.

His jaw tight, Patrick changed the subject. "So now we drive back to my apartment. I give you a simple good-night kiss and get out of the car, then you go on home. Right?"

Baffled by his uncharacteristically gruff tone, she hedged, "That was the plan. Wasn't it?" Considering how he'd acted earlier, she had expected him to invite her into his apartment, and they'd do far more than kiss. However, now she had serious doubts about accepting the invitation or that it would even be extended.

"That was the plan," he repeated, gritting his teeth. You have to plan everything and keep to it, he told himself. Do things *properly*! The words he directed toward Blythe were entirely different. "I suppose you have to be at the courthouse early?"

"My first case is scheduled at nine."

Blythe's brows rose as Patrick pressed down on the gas pedal, and the car shot around a sharp curve in the street. "That's twelve hours from now, McBride. There's no need to speed."

Without slowing down he asked, "You've got a full schedule this week?"

"Yes," Blythe replied. "Don't you?"

He answered with a grunt and followed up with an equally disgruntled demand, "So I suppose you think I should call you next weekend when you're free and invite you out to dinner or something?"

"Is that what you want to do?"

To Blythe, Patrick's indifferent shrug seemed more like a condemnation of her than a response to her question. The glance he shot her was cold, but he said nothing more, leaving Blythe completely baffled. Evidently, somewhere between the time when they'd sat down to dinner with his family and the time his mother had extended her sincere wish for Blythe to come back and visit them again, Patrick had questioned the wisdom of becoming involved with her.

Having no idea what could have prompted his doubts and forgetting that she still had several of her own, Blythe replayed the whole evening in her mind. From all indications Patrick was in a fine old temper over something. What might she have said or done to set him off?

She recalled a short after-dinner conversation, the only awkward moments in the otherwise enjoyable hours she'd spent with his family. Patrick's mother had asked him if he would be making his routine stop at the Stag's Head Bar Monday night or if he had other plans. He'd looked to Blythe as if expecting her to answer for him. Since they'd made no plans to meet after work, she had said nothing, and Patrick had scowled at her as if she'd somehow let him down.

What should she have done? Invited herself along? Answered for Patrick?

Patrick wasn't the sort of man anyone led. Blythe hadn't felt she had the right to plan his social engagements. Even agreeing to a get-together with his family was overstepping his tolerance. As far as she was concerned, the question hadn't been hers to answer.

Caught up in her own thoughts, Blythe practically jumped out of her skin when Patrick burst out, "Why must you always be so damned methodical, Cramer? It makes me crazy!" That said, he turned off into an alley, sped into a parking lot behind a ten-story brick building and braked to a stop. "This is my building."

Through clenched teeth, she inquired evenly, "Are you going to explain that remark, McBride, or am I expected to read your mind?"

Instead of answering, Patrick got out of the car and strode around to her side. He pulled open the door and reached for her arm. "C'mon. We'll discuss this inside."

"Discuss what? My being methodical?" Evidently his changeable mind had decided to forgo the good-night kiss in the car and the quick farewell. Against her better judgment she allowed herself to be assisted from the car and hustled across the parking lot. Within seconds she was out of breath. "Did you and your brothers have some kind of training in commandeering women like this, or does it come naturally?"

"What?" Patrick slowed down enough to realize she was having difficulty keeping pace and immediately loosened his hold on her arm. "Sorry. I wasn't thinking."

Blythe gave him a look that said she doubted he had much of anything cerebral to think with, but instead of provoking him it made him laugh. "You do bring out the caveman in me, sweetheart."

"As I said this afternoon, sometimes you're not that far removed from your primate cousins," she replied, letting her annoyance color her tone.

Chuckling, Patrick resumed walking, matching his stride to hers. "At least I didn't haul you out of the car by the hair and drag you off to my lair.

"Not that I'm not tempted. There's a lot to be said for primitive passion. Back in the Stone Age, a man didn't have to waste so much of his time convincing his woman. A hundred thousand years ago, I could have stripped off all your clothes, thrown you down on a pile of fur robes and made love to you all day and night without you questioning all the social ramifications."

"Ugh," Blythe retorted in a way even a Stone-Age man would understand.

A smile played at the corners of Patrick's mouth as he watched her trying to get her erratic breathing under control. "Be careful," he warned her softly as he opened the wide oak door and placed a hand at the small of her back to guide her inside the building. "Your body keeps trying to tell me you're not that adverse to the idea."

"Don't be ridiculous," Blythe scoffed even as a wave of sensual heat turned her cheeks a bright pink. She stepped away from his touch and was halfway down the hall before she realized Patrick was no longer behind her. More flustered than ever, she turned around and found him leaning against the wall, pointing at the door of the elevator. Her defiant expression told him he'd better not say another word as she retraced her steps and walked ahead of him into the small enclosed space.

With his back to her, Patrick closed the metal grate and the heavy doors slid shut. He pressed the button for the tenth floor, then slowly turned around to face her. He looked utterly dangerous as he said conversationally, "This is an old building."

"It's charming." Blythe swallowed hard, sensing something predatory in his gaze.

"Very old." He moved toward her. "This elevator takes an age to get to the top."

"That must be frustrating at times."

Patrick advanced and Blythe backed up until her shoulders were against the wall. Her mouth went dry as he placed a hand on either side of her body.

"Uh-huh," Patrick agreed silkily, lowering his head until his mouth was a whisper away from her lips. "But not half as frustrating as wanting to kiss you without the eyes of the world upon us. Kiss me, Blythe," he ordered huskily, pressing his lower body against her softness so she could feel how badly he wanted her. "Show me how much you've been wanting the same thing."

Blythe caught her breath as the hardness of his body enticed her, and the temptation of his lips drew her. Maybe she was a methodical person, but keeping up with his mood swings was sometimes beyond her. Who was making whom crazy here?

Patrick brushed his lips across Blythe's, then back again.

She kept her lips sealed in a tight line and concentrated all her will on remaining unresponsive. She'd show him that her feelings weren't as changeable as his. A person didn't drop one mood and jump into the next in the length of time it took to snap your fingers.

Patrick flicked the tip of his tongue across her lips.

Blythe closed her eyes and whimpered softly. She tried to shrink back against the elevator wall, but instead she swayed forward. Evidently craziness was infectious, and she'd caught his.

What else could explain why her hands rose to curl over the back of his neck? Given that there was some unresolved problem between them, misunderstandings still to be explained, she was insane to open her lips over his, but she was doing just that.

As her tongue delved inside him and her fingers slid down his shoulders to his chest, his breathing grew more and more labored. Deciding that if she was slipping into insanity, she wasn't going alone, she grasped hold of the lapels of his jacket. She pulled him closer as the familiar all-consuming hunger took over.

Holding nothing back, she tasted him with a desire that only increased as his mouth crushed down on her lips and his tongue met hers. At some point the enticer became the enticed, and as Patrick took control of their kiss, she began to ache for the feel of his hands on her. Her body demanded the kind of pleasure only he could give. "Patrick," she moaned. "I do want you."

Patrick raised his head as the elevator door slid open. "And I you," he murmured unsteadily. His smile was sweet as he took her hand and drew her down the carpeted hallway to his apartment. He took the key from his pocket and inserted it in the lock, but before the door opened, his mouth was on hers again.

Blythe didn't realize they were inside until he lifted her into his arms and began walking through a large living room. Patrick reached down and turned on a small brass lamp as they passed a rolltop desk, and Blythe was able to gain a glimpse of the room as he strode through it. An overstuffed couch in rust suede, two brown leather chairs, a tan brick fireplace: all very masculine.

Some shred of sanity remained, and Blythe's innate sense of order surfaced. "I thought we were coming in here to discuss something."

"Later."

"About my date last night—"

"I don't want to hear about it."

"I had dinner with Judge Abernathy and his wife."

Patrick halted their progress and glared down at her. "Why didn't you tell me that in the first place? I wouldn't have spent all last night thinking about you and some other man."

"Did you think about me all last night?" she asked, twirling the tip of her finger around the outer edge of his ear.

"Yes, I thought about you all last night," Patrick admitted curtly. "You've become an obsession with me, lady."

"Have I really?" She trailed her fingertips down his neck and followed around the edge of his collar, exploring this new talent for teasing.

"You have."

He lifted her higher, and Blythe tightened her arms around his neck. The delicate scent of roses drifted upward, and Patrick was enveloped by it. His expression softened as his gaze centered on her mouth. Blythe purposely ran the tip of her tongue over her lips. Patrick groaned and lowered his head.

Covering her mouth with his own, he kissed her with masterful dominance, tasting, exploring and establishing his claim. For once Blythe was unable to challenge him and was content to follow. At some point during the kiss, Patrick started moving down the short hall-way. As he lifted his lips from hers, he pushed a door open with his shoulder.

Shakily Blythe managed to tease, "Is this what you call a simple good-night kiss?"

"Nothing's ever simple with you," he muttered as he flipped on a light and continued carrying her into the room.

His bedroom was decorated in strong, vibrant colors, the perfect setting for a strong, vibrant man. The bed was dark oak and king-size with a colorful woven Mexican spread. Indian rugs were scattered across the wide-plank wood floor. The dresser, chest, bookshelves and chair were also of oak, giving the room a comfortable, sturdy look.

"I'm going to make love to you, and there's not going to be anything simple about that, either," Patrick announced as he pulled aside the spread and laid her down. "The last time, everything happened so fast. This time I want it to be slow. I want to watch you, look into your eyes when I touch you and see the expression on your face when I'm inside you."

He removed his jacket and tie. "And I want to feel your eyes on me." Slowly he unbuttoned his shirt and stripped it off.

Willingly Blythe granted his wish as she watched him undress. The last time they'd been together had been too fast to indulge in the sight of each other. This time they could, and she was fascinated. His chest was broad, his skin golden and gleaming. When he stood before her nude, she almost cried out with the need to touch such male perfection, the powerful muscles of his chest, his flat stomach and strong thighs. When he came to her, he took such an agonizingly long time removing her clothes that she could no longer contain herself. His insistence that they go slowly seemed an absolute impossibility as she took his weight upon herself, arching her body in delight.

"Please," she pleaded, twisting beneath him, completely aroused by his kisses, his words and the promise of his body.

With a groan, he denied her, seeking to know more, needing to find all the places that gave her the most pleasure. The only time he was sure of her and was positive that she couldn't deny what they shared any more than he could was when they were making love. This time he would make certain she wouldn't deny it even if a hundred years passed before they came together again.

Blythe was a logical thinker, but there was no logic in what had happened between them. To prove to her that they belonged together, he would have to make sure she forgot to think until it was too late. Otherwise he feared she might think herself right out of his life. A day, a week, the short amount of time they'd spent in rediscovery shouldn't matter, considering what they'd found out. They couldn't even call it love at first sight since they'd been in each other's thoughts for years. Time wasn't important.

Blythe had to realize that nothing was more important than what they felt for each other, even if others might not see things the same way. Liberal, conservative, lawyer, judge, Democrat, Republican—they were still a perfect match. Didn't she understand why she exploded in his arms? Before this night was over, Blythe was going to admit that she loved him.

Patrick fought desperately to maintain his control as his mouth and hands explored every soft, luscious inch of her. On his quest he discovered that the creamy skin beneath her collarbone was particularly sensitive to his touch, that she whimpered with longing when he teased her nipples with his tongue. Her slender legs quivered beneath his lips. She felt like rose petals all over, but there was nothing fragile or tender about the passionate creature she became when he kissed the most delicate parts of her body.

It was then that her response overwhelmed him. Her eyes went wild, an intense beautiful blue that blazed into his. Her body trembled, shuddered beneath him, around him, above him. He was surrounded by Blythe, and he felt as savage as any male who strives for dominance over a woman who matches him on every possible level.

He caught her wrists before she could take what was hers and pressed them down beside her head, grateful that his strength had not completely deserted him. He watched her face as he entered her, saw the satisfaction in her smile as he tried once to withdraw before accepting her advance and found he could not. He belonged to this woman, and his body refused to do without her for another second.

"God! How I love you," he groaned mindlessly, in defeat and triumph as he lost himself in her.

Blythe felt the mounting tremors inside herself and in him. With abandoned joy she moaned his name over and over again. When her hands were released from his hold, she slid her arms around his waist, drawing him more deeply into her.

He loved her. Patrick loved her, her brain shouted the words as her body arched in fierce pleasure and the tension rose to the breaking point. Release came in a series of blinding explosions, then reverberated down into the breathless moments of exhausted fulfillment.

For Blythe it was like dying and being reborn into a world of exquisite wonder. She savored each miraculous sensation, made even more acute by the sensitized nerve endings that tingled beneath her skin. Patrick was draped over her like a warm living blanket.

His breath was mingled with hers, his dark auburn hair soft against her throat. She felt the brush of his lashes on her cheek, the touch of his lips on the lobe of her ear. This was her man who had just accompanied her to paradise. Hers to love, and she most certainly did.

She was stunned as she realized the impetuous conclusion she had just reached. She realized that she wanted to spend the rest of her life with this man. He drove her crazy, but it was craziness she didn't want to live without.

Loving the feel of him, she relived the past few minutes in her mind. Had he really meant what he'd said to her? Did he love her, too, or had he spoken the words in reaction to the uncontrollable passion that had overtaken them both in those final seconds before completion? Even as her body drifted into a contented languor at the thought of Patrick loving her, her mind rejected the possibility of there being any truth in his passion-laden declaration.

It was too soon, too improbable. But then, when did Patrick do anything reasonable? Or when did she react predictably in his arms?

"Patrick?" Gently she shook his arm. "Patrick, did you mean what you said?"

Patrick lifted his head, met her clear-eyed gaze and swallowed a groan. Before she could interpret his love-sick expression, he slid off her and rolled onto his back. No way was he prepared to answer her question.

Staring up at the ceiling, he called himself all sorts of names, the kindest one being fool. He'd blown it, really blown it. He wasn't supposed to come up out of a sensual stupor and realize he'd made a declaration of love. She was supposed to have done that.

Rolling to his side, he propped his head on his elbow and forced a grin. "Of course. What do you think we just did? Made like?"

Blythe stared at the wall beyond his ear, fearing her reaction if she met his twinkling gaze head-on. His denial was clear. Disappointment flooded through her. She swallowed, then quickly picked up her pride. Faking a laugh, she scoffed, "Made like? You're a born comedian, McBride."

He leaned over her and pressed kisses into the smooth flesh of her shoulder. "Yep, old keep 'em laughing McBride, that's me. Lord, you taste good. I think I'm addicted to roses and satin. That's what you are, you know."

He kissed along the line of her collarbone, dipped his tongue into the hollow of her neck, then resumed kissing his way to her other shoulder. "Roses. Always roses. I think you smelled like roses in the first grade."

Adding more ammunition to the gentle assault on her nerve endings, Patrick traced a swirling design down her side with his fingertips. He nuzzled her ear, then teased the ultrasensitive spot behind it with the tip of his tongue. Blythe squirmed. "Patrick..."

His fingers had made the return trip and grazed the bottom slope of her breast. Blythe caught his hand and stilled its movement. "I should go home."

"Stay all night." He released his hand from her capture, reached for the edge of the top sheet and pulled it up over them.

"I can't do that." She pushed away the sheet and started to get up before the temptation to remain in his arms grew any stronger.

"Can't or won't?" he demanded as he sat up and watched her gather up her clothing.

"They're one and the same," she muttered as she stepped into her silk-and-lace teddy.

"Aha! Gotcha! *Can't* implies being physically unable or in some way prevented, whereas *won't* implies the exercise of one's individual will, a choice."

"Spare me," Blythe mumbled from behind the linen she was slipping over her head. "I picked up the fine points of Dr. Leslie's famous lecture on courtroom cross-examination, too. The semantics are immaterial. I'm leaving, and I'd rather go now than at five or six in the morning."

"You wouldn't have to leave that early, you know. Your apartment is only four blocks away. You could go around seven-thirty and still have plenty of time to change and get to your office by nine."

Blythe's frown warned Patrick what she thought of that idea even before she said, "Oh, sure, and announce to scores of people in your building and mine that we've spent the night together. I may not be the most recognizable public official, but there's bound to be some who'd know me. I can't afford to take that chance."

Realizing that with each garment that Blythe replaced his chances of enticing her back to bed went down, Patrick rolled off the mattress. On the way to his closet for a robe, he said, "All the more reason why I should move in with you."

Irritated that she couldn't find her second shoe, Blythe stomped lopsidedly around the room as she searched. "Don't start that again, McBride."

Totally unconcerned with his own nudity, Patrick clutched his robe in one hand and her shoe in the other. "This what you're looking for?" he asked, holding the slender pump.

He jerked it out of her reach as she reached for it. Blythe fell against Patrick's chest, and he quickly curled his arms around her to keep her there. "If you won't let me move in with you, I assume the reverse is true?" He waited for her nod of affirmation.

"Then we have three choices left. A: we call it quits right now. No good, because we can't. B: we have a discreet affair. C: we get married."

"Get married?" She leaned away from him and saw his grinning face. Obviously he didn't consider the last a real choice.

"Yeah, how about this week?"

Matching his flippant tone, she quipped, "Sorry, my calendar is full. This week's out."

"Okay, too soon. You'd need time to buy a new dress, anyway. How about next week?"

Blythe pushed herself out of his arms, unable to continue joking about something that would never happen, no matter how much she wanted it to. She grabbed her shoe before he could move it out of reach again and slipped it on her foot. Hiding her hurt, she tossed off, "Get serious, McBride."

Patrick didn't try to pull her back into his arms. He'd tested the waters and found Blythe wasn't ready to make a permanent commitment. But he wasn't going to let her leave without some assurance that she hadn't opted for plan A. "You'll agree that there's something between us that we can't ignore, won't you?"

Blythe tensed, then turned back to look at the unabashedly nude male who was questioning her. Even if she wanted to evade answering, the smoldering heat in her eyes as she viewed his glorious nakedness gave her away. Sighing, she admitted, "Yes, there is. What do you think we should do about it?"

Patrick's eyes narrowed on her. "I gave you three options. You're the judge. Make a decision."

She didn't respond for a long time. Patrick was almost certain she was about to tell him to go take a flying leap when she calmly announced, "A discreet affair seems the best solution for both parties in this case. Agreed?"

"Agreed."

Ten

Blythe unhooked her judicial robe as she dropped onto the big comfortable chair behind her desk. Closing her eyes, she leaned back against the supple leather. Tipping her head slowly from side to side, she eased the kinks out of her neck. It had been a long afternoon. Child custody battles were always painful to deal with, and she'd had two such cases in one day.

"At least you've got a treat to finish off the day on a happy note," Leona informed her as she whisked into the office.

Her eyes still closed, Blythe smiled, remembering the next appointment on her calendar. Today would mark the final step in the adoption of two brothers and a sister by a very special couple with enough love to open their hearts to a ready-made family. "The Sheltons," she said, her smile widening. "I'm looking forward to it. I far prefer creating families to dividing them up."

"And that's not all you've got waiting for you," Leona commented. "This came while you were in court."

Blythe opened her eyes and watched her secretary place a square white box, tied with an emerald green ribbon, on her desk. "It doesn't tick, does it?" she asked jokingly as she eyed the twelve cubic-inch container.

"Nope. I even gave it a shake, just in case. But I'll call the bomb squad if you want," Leona volunteered, tongue-in-cheek.

It was a long-standing joke of theirs that one of her decisions might someday anger someone enough that they'd want to get back at her. Decisions handed down by the judges of domestic courts didn't usually incite violent reactions, but she'd be naive to ignore the possibility. Therefore she always exercised some caution when receiving unexpected packages.

Giving the box one last suspicious look, Blythe reached for the ribbon and slipped it off. "Stand back, Leona. No telling what might jump out at us."

Nothing did. When the lid had been off for a precautionary second or two, Blythe peeped inside. Smiling up at her was a reddish-brown stuffed monkey with a small envelope taped to his chest. It didn't take Blythe long to figure out who had sent it.

Patrick had been full of "monkey business" for the past two weeks. He'd carried her insistence that their affair be discreet to the extreme. In an effort to point out how ridiculous he thought her fears, he'd taken to wearing ludicrous disguises each time he came or went from her apartment. When he phoned her at work, he gave Leona a false name. So far this week, she'd received calls from Robert Redford, George Washington and the president of the United States.

Patrick had gone to hilarious lengths to keep their association a secret. He even made arrangements for their nightly "rendezvous" through coded messages that turned up on her desk at odd times during the day. They were signed "a secret admirer."

Leona claimed not to have read any after finding the first, which she'd deemed completely undecipherable. Blythe hoped that her secretary had yet to break Patrick's mysterious codes, for his notes related more than time and destination. References to how their evening together would end were often sizzling.

Blythe hesitated as she looked at his latest message, fearing what might be in the note and at the same time feeling a rush of pleasure. She reached for the envelope and held it in her palm, almost expecting to be burned by touching it.

"A stuffed toy?" Leona asked, completely puzzled until she saw the Mona Lisa smile on her boss's face. "Your secret admirer wouldn't be Patrick McBride, would it?"

Blythe couldn't suppress the startled gurgle that erupted from her throat. "Ah...uh...what makes you think that?"

"Elementary, my dear Watson," Leona proclaimed loftily as she pointed at the cuddly stuffed toy. "The resemblance is unmistakable. So open the note."

Leaning forward in anticipation, Leona adjusted her glasses. "Let's see if he used a code I can figure out this time. I've been dying to know what he's been writing."

Amazed by the woman's easy acceptance of Patrick as her admirer, Blythe looked from the sealed envelope to her secretary and back again. Judging by the woman's dreamy smile, she appeared to approve of her boss's romantic involvement with a zany member of the political opposition, but Blythe still didn't think it wise to admit how deep that involvement went. She wasn't sure herself, at least not on Patrick's behalf, and until he was ready to make a commitment, the fewer people who knew of their affair, the better.

As far as she could tell, Patrick was satisfied with things as they were. His only complaint was that she stubbornly refused to conduct their affair out in the open. Was she being a prude, as he implied? No, she firmly believed that discretion was the better part of valor, and she had far more to lose than he did if word got out that they were living together. Still, even if they were to continue as they were, their relationship couldn't be kept secret much longer.

Blythe swallowed the frustration she felt whenever she contemplated her present situation, realizing that Leona was still waiting for her to reveal the contents of Patrick's note. "Don't you have some documents to gather up for me before the Sheltons get here?"

Leona tapped a manila folder placed in the center of Blythe's desk. "Already done and waiting, Your Honor." With a flippant grin, she patted an imaginary stray hair into place and announced, "If you need to be alone, I suppose I could find something that calls for my immediate attention in the outer office."

"Do that."

Sighing with disappointment, Leona stepped back, but offered, "If you need any help figuring out what he says, my keen powers of deduction are at your disposal."

"Thanks, but I'll try to muddle through on my own."

Leona sailed toward the doorway but was unable to resist one parting shot. "Patrick McBride is a good match for you, even if he is a *Democrat*." She whispered the last word as if the walls around her might fall down if she said it aloud.

"Go answer the phone or something," Blythe ordered with mock sternness, though her eyes shone with affection.

The unopened envelope still lay in Blythe's hand. For another moment she stared at it. What was Patrick up to this time? Finally she broke the seal and pulled the card out. Patrick's handwriting was unmistakable, and Blythe's fingertips moved unconsciously to the very edge of the card as she held it.

Dinner at seven—Fireworks to follow—*All* night long—What kind they are is up to you.
                              The Monkey's cousin

Frowning, Blythe stared at the message for a moment. Since he'd begun this craziness, she'd cracked everything from pig Latin to Morse code, but this time the words were in plain English. Patrick was delivering an ultimatum that she couldn't misinterpret. He was planning to spend the entire night with her, rather than sneak down the back stairs some time before dawn, as he had been doing. If she had a problem with that, she'd better be prepared for a fight.

Blythe kissed the card and grinned. So Patrick was just as frustrated with the present state of affairs as she was. He was in for a big surprise if he thought she'd offer any resistance to his spending an entire night in her bed. She'd like nothing better. She wanted all of his nights and his days, too.

She was in love with him, hopelessly, thoroughly, disgustingly in love. Each time he left her, she yearned to call him back, tell him that she wouldn't care what anyone thought if she could trust that her feelings for him were returned. If nothing else, the past two weeks had irrevocably proved to her that she wanted to be with him for the rest of her life. She didn't even want to think about the boring and lonely life she had been leading before he came back into it.

Patrick might make her lose the iron grip she'd always kept on her temper more often than anyone, but he also made her laugh. He admired her professional capabilities, respected what he considered her superior intellect, but could also lavish her body with such ardent attention that she wondered if her brainpower mattered to him at all. Even more amazing, his attitude pleased her immensely, rather than insulted her. All her life she'd been looking for a man who wanted both body and brains in a woman. Patrick Donovan McBride was that man.

Blythe read his card again and contemplated the astounding changes Patrick had wrought in her. Because of him, the Honorable Judge Cramer, upstanding citizen and staid representative of the conservative party, was fast becoming addicted to dazzling displays of sensual fervor. Just this morning, when she'd seen a veiled reference to herself and Patrick in Bob Whittiker's gossip column, she'd surprised herself by being more amused than angry. After admitting that she'd fallen in love with an outspoken liberal, she'd undergone hours of self-analysis and realized that she'd rather lose in the next election than give up Patrick. Somehow she was going to have to prove that to him.

Glancing down at his card, she savored thoughts of the coming evening. A few seconds later she slipped the card back into its envelope, lest the suggestion of the impending fireworks exploded in her hand. Images of exactly what kind of fireworks Patrick hoped to inspire were already beginning to explode inside her body. Every time he touched her, even looked at her, she went off like a Roman candle.

She tossed the envelope back into the box and replaced the lid, wishing she could tuck away thoughts of Patrick just as easily. Instead of wondering if and when he'd ever come to love her as she loved him, she needed to concentrate on the documents Leona had prepared for the Sheltons' adoption ceremony. Blythe wanted this proceeding to go through without a hitch. The three lovely children and Barbara and Jerry Shelton deserved nothing less.

Picking up the folder, Blythe started reading the caseworker's report. It was a very complimentary report, concluding with a wholehearted recommendation that the Sheltons be allowed to adopt the three Nelson siblings.

Recent pictures of the children were included with the report, and Blythe took the time to study them. All three were blond and blue-eyed; the relationship between them unmistakable. Looking at their smiling faces, aglow with health and happiness, it was hard to believe that they were the same sick, malnourished orphans whose sad plight had been pictured in the papers last winter.

Remembering the details of the case, Blythe shuddered. Their father was dead, had been killed in an auto accident a year before the children had lost their mother. From details pieced together by the police, it appeared that Celia Nelson, totally distraught over her husband's death, had fallen easy victim to a man who came to be her lover. What little money she might have had, had gone to support the man's drug habit, and the young family's situation had rapidly spiraled downward. The woman's battered body had been found in the trunk of her car. Her lover had been picked up in a neighboring state and was presently serving a life sentence for murder.

Fortunately this tragic story was going to have a happy ending. The Sheltons had opened their home and hearts to the three frightened, withdrawn and very sick children. After today they would no longer have to worry about the children, whom they now loved as their own, being taken away from them.

Blythe felt a tug of envy as she pictured the outcome of the adoption proceedings. In a few minutes the Sheltons could consider themselves a real family. Until Patrick, Blythe hadn't realized how deeply she yearned to have a husband and children of her own. Until him, she hadn't realized what kind of sacrifices she'd made to achieve her career goals. In her pursuit of a career in law, she'd forgone all else. Her personal life had been practically nonexistent. But Patrick had shown her that her judicial robes wouldn't be able to keep her warm at night. When she stepped down from the bench, she needed someone to be waiting. With all of her heart she prayed that Patrick would be that someone.

Maybe tonight she'd work up her courage and admit that she wanted to have more with him than a discreet little affair. What would he do then? Tell her he loved her, wanted to marry her, or take off on a dead run?

Leona buzzed her on the intercom, and Blythe was thankful for the interruption. For the next hour her thoughts were completely occupied with the adoption proceedings. Blythe employed the same procedure her uncle had in making the affair a ceremony—almost like a wedding—where the parents and children repeated vows. Once the final papers were signed, Leona produced a small cake and a pitcher of fruit punch to celebrate the creation of a new family. It was a happy note to end the day, and the happiest of all ways to close what had started as a very tragic case. Blythe could only hope her own situation would be resolved as happily.

Over Leona's protestations, Blythe helped clear up the office after the party, then gathered up her purse and briefcase. She was almost through the door when Leona stopped her.

"Aren't you forgetting something?" Leona asked, a smirk of mischief lighting her face as she handed Blythe the white box that had been shoved aside and forgotten for the past hour. "I suspect you'd rather take this little monkey home, that is, unless you intend to perch him somewhere here in the office." She glanced at her watch. "Hmmm...it's almost six. You'd better get a move on so you can have some time to freshen up before you see that charming devil tonight."

Blythe eyed her secretary with suspicion. "Just where are you getting all your information?"

"I have my sources," Leona returned mysteriously. She gave Blythe a little shove out the door. "Get going, Your Honor."

Having no choice, Blythe did get going, and a short while later was walking through her apartment door. She had an hour to prepare for Patrick's arrival, an hour to think about the best way to approach him with her feelings. It was also enough time to soak her tired body in a warm tub of bubbly water.

She was just stepping out of the tub when the doorbell rang. There was no doubt in her mind as to the identity of her caller, just as there was no doubt that he wouldn't go away if she ignored the summons. "You're early, McBride," she complained as she stepped into a hooded terry robe and zipped it up to her chin.

They met at the door. Patrick craned his head from behind the two large white bags he carried. "Hello, darlin'. Are you hungry?" Without really looking at Blythe, he sped past her. Halfway down the hall, he turned on his heel, dropped a small duffel bag onto the floor, then returned to where Blythe was still standing.

Leaning down, he planted a quick kiss on her lips, then hurried away again in the general direction of her kitchen. "I had a helluva day. I thought we'd stay here for dinner. We can eat right out the cartons so we won't have to mess up your kitchen. Do you like Chinese?"

Blythe followed him to the kitchen, crossed her arms in front of her chest and leaned against the doorframe. It was hard to keep a straight face. Patrick was acting as if he were as nervous about this evening as she was. Was he that worried that she'd refuse to let him spend the night with her? Was it possible that he'd fallen in love with her as she had with him, but doubted that his feelings were returned? What if she came right out and admitted how she felt before he made his stand?

Blythe considered doing that for a moment, then realized he was waiting impatiently for an answer. Seeing his dark scowl, she lost her courage. Her throat was tight, and her words sounded less than genial. "Would it make any difference if I didn't?"

Oops! Patrick grimaced inwardly, turning his back on her as he emptied the cartons from the bags. "I'll have to eat it all if you don't." Out of the corner of his eye, he dared another glance at her. She didn't look any too happy with him. Had he gone too far with that ultimatum? Been too peremptory?

This was the first time he'd come openly prepared to spend the night, but since they'd been together every evening for the past two weeks, it had seemed silly to ask for her permission. His ego had taken enough of a beating when she'd adamantly refused to discuss their living together. He'd done everything possible to show her that her attitude was old-fashioned, paranoid and immature, but it was beginning to look as if she was perfectly content with things as they were. Well, he wasn't.

Blythe wasn't the only one who had principles. Patrick knew she ran her life with a strict moral code, analyzing everything according to the rules, the fairness and rightness of an action. That's why she made such a good judge, but she wasn't playing fair here. Right was on his side. They belonged together, and he'd felt that sooner or later she would come to recognize that.

To protect his own integrity, Patrick had decided it was going to be sooner. More and more often lately he'd begun to wonder if putting his heart completely out on the limb, begging her to marry him wouldn't be worth the gamble. But then he'd tell himself that she had enough to contend with as it was. Allowing him to intrude on her well-ordered life as much as he already had was a step in the right direction. Unfortunately he didn't have the patience to wait for her to take another step. He was through skulking out of her apartment in the wee hours of the morning.

He'd given the matter a lot of thought. Although he was scared to death by the possible outcome, he was determined to make a stand. He couldn't go on this way any longer. If Blythe didn't love him by now, she never would. If she didn't think he was good enough for her, it was time for her to admit it. He wanted the whole world to know how he felt, and if she didn't feel the same way, it was over.

Blythe heaved away from the doorframe and toward the row of cupboards behind Patrick. The sound of her voice made him jump. "I insist we use plates and regular silverware. I don't mind putting them in the dishwasher, and I'm too tired to struggle with chopsticks. I had a hard day, too."

Patrick's expression was all concern as he wrapped his arms around her. "Always glad to accommodate the bench." Unable to resist the vulnerability in her large blue eyes, he kissed her, his mouth open and slanted across hers. It was a mind-stealing kiss and Blythe could barely stand when he lifted his lips from hers.

"Lord, I needed that," Patrick muttered as he skimmed kisses over her face. "Put your arms around me, Blythe. I need that, too."

Blythe did as he asked, sliding her arms around his waist as Patrick tightened his hold on her. He rested his cheek against the top of her head and hauled her closer, seemingly desperate. "Patrick?" Blythe asked. She smoothed her hands soothingly across his back. "What's wrong?"

"Nothing," he lied. "This is exactly what I needed to keep my mind off other things." He breathed deeply of her scent. "All clean, fresh and smelling of roses."

Intuitively Blythe asked, "Bad case?"

"So rotten it stinks," he said as he loosened his hold, glad he had something to talk about that might explain the strange mood he was in. It also allowed him for a little while longer to put off a discussion he dreaded.

Memorizing the feel of her skin, he brushed his lips across her forehead. "I turned down a fat fee because there was no way I wanted to feel responsible for putting a real scumbag back on the street."

Blythe had a good idea what case Patrick was talking about. The evening before, a local businessman, well-known for his work with young people, had been taken into custody and accused of being the kingpin in a narcotics and child-prostitution ring. The case was big, and the public was highly emotional about it. The ring had targeted schools, especially elementary and junior highs. "The Rico case."

Patrick nodded. "Just to be fair, I spent most of the day going over the details, but..." He dropped his arms from around her and slammed his fist on the counter. "Damn! I know he's supposed to be innocent until proven guilty, but if he's not found guilty, there's no such thing as justice."

"Lawyers don't take the Hippocratic oath—you can turn away a possible client."

"But we're not supposed to judge them, just argue their case." He whirled around, his eyes cold and determined.

This was a side of Patrick that Blythe hadn't seen. Even as impassioned as he'd become during the Wynbush case, he hadn't been like this. No wonder he was known as a crusader for the rights of the downtrodden. He was so intense, so fervent in his zeal for justice.

"I'd like to be the prosecuting attorney or the judge and sentence that bastard to spend the rest of his life in prison. How do you do it, Blythe? How do you keep your emotions out of your decisions?"

"You're forgetting that in a case like this, a jury will decide whether he's innocent or guilty," she reminded him calmly. "The judge will determine only the sentence."

"But a judge could sway the jury with a few words or by allowing one of the attorneys to step beyond the bounds of proper procedure," he maintained.

"The judge could, and some have, but they're not supposed to," Blythe returned, feeling slightly uncomfortable. Suddenly it felt as if Patrick were grilling her about something that had nothing to do with their present topic of conversation. "Personal feelings are supposed to be put aside. A good judge should be able to do that."

"And you're a very good judge, aren't you, Blythe Cramer?" he probed bitterly. "You can turn your emotions on and off as if you had a switch inside you."

"How can *you*, of all people, say that?" she asked, hurt by his unfair attack. "All you do is flit from one emotion to the next like a jumping jack. I never know where I stand with you. In the past two weeks I really thought we were getting to know each other."

Patrick gave her a cutting look. "That just shows how little you must care. If you felt anything for me at all, you'd have realized that I expected more to come out of this affair than having a warm body in my bed. I can get that anywhere."

"What else were you expecting?" Blythe demanded, hoping they had finally reached the moment of truth and that he was going to tell her he loved her, and mean it.

What else was I expecting? Patrick repeated her question silently, enraged that she had to ask. Obviously she hadn't expected anything but what they already had. "Forget it!" he bit out. "I know now that no matter what I do I'll never get through to the Iron

Maiden. You're as cold and unfeeling as everyone says.''

Blythe had heard the name before, but coming from Patrick's lips, it had never been more insulting. She marched over to him, placed her hands on his cheeks, pulled down his face and gave him a toe-curling kiss. ''How's that for unfeeling?''

Patrick's green eyes flamed like sulfurous fire. ''All you think about is sex! That's all you've ever wanted from me, isn't it? I told you I loved you. I asked you to marry me, and what did you offer in return? A sleazy back street affair!''

In a rendition of his most flamboyant courtroom dramatics, he paced the kitchen, gesturing wildly as he ranted, ''Well, I'm sick of it! I'm sick of being nothing but a sex object. I refuse to be your kept man.''

Blythe's joy was so great that it was bubbling over. She had no idea when he thought he'd told her he loved her and proposed marriage, but she didn't care as long as he still felt the same way. ''Patrick, this is ridiculous and totally unnecessary,'' she shouted to be heard. Unfortunately he misunderstood the motive behind her interruption.

Rounding on her, Patrick bellowed, ''Forgive me, Your Honor, for my unseemly display of emotion. Us lesser types not only have feelings, but we express them. Since you don't have any, you probably can't understand that. Well, you may not want to hear this, but you're damned well going to. You've been bleeding me dry for two weeks. No, correct that. Thirty years! I've given you that long to realize that I'm the man for you, but I'm not butting my head against your steel armor one more second. I'm through!''

"Patrick, please. Will you just listen to me for a moment?" Blythe pleaded, realizing he was planning to leave without giving her a chance to defend herself.

"Spare me," Patrick countered sarcastically with words she had once used on him. "I can't afford to take the chance that you'll talk me back into your bed. I gave you my heart, Blythe Cramer, but I've still got some pride left, and I'm not a fool. I'm leaving before you can stomp all over it again."

He stormed out of the kitchen, and Blythe ran after him. "Patrick McBride, you come back here!"

Patrick ignored her order, and before she could stop him, he had slammed the door in her face. She stood gaping for a long moment, then slowly recovered her wits. As she considered all that had just transpired, her shoulders began to shake with laughter. "The idiot left before I could tell him I love him."

Shaking her head, she turned away from the door, still smiling. Patrick would make a lousy judge. He just didn't take the time to listen to both sides of an argument. She was going to have to take drastic measures in order to make sure he heard the case for the defense.

Eleven

By nine o'clock Patrick was on his fourth drink. It was Friday night, so the Stag's Head wouldn't be closing until one in the morning. If his family possessed enough wisdom to stay off his back, that gave him more than enough time to completely drown his sorrows. His coordination was already off. When he picked up his glass for another swallow, he had difficulty finding his mouth.

Unfortunately, his brain was still functioning. He was insanely in love with Blythe Cramer, but, thanks to his stupid temper, their relationship was over. He hadn't meant to attack her that way, but when had he ever shown any finesse in dealing with her? Not tonight, that was for sure. His feelings for her were too strong, too elemental, and that had placed him in an indefensible position.

A man couldn't subordinate himself to Blythe without losing her respect. Continuing their affair when the feelings involved were so one-sided would eventually have accomplished the same thing he had accomplished tonight with his hotheaded speech, but at least their breakup would have been more dignified. It was just that loving her had put him in a no-win situation.

For two weeks he'd danced to her tune, praying she would come to the same conclusions he had—that an affair would never be enough for them. For some, two weeks probably wouldn't seem a long time. For him, it had been an eternity.

With every day that had passed, Blythe had seemed more and more content to leave things as they were. He had to believe, even if he had made a total fool out of himself in the process, that he'd been right to force the issue. He'd found out that no matter what amount of time he'd given her, it wouldn't have made any difference. Two weeks, two months or two years, her feelings would never match his.

He lifted his glass and grumbled, "Ah, pride, the never-failing vice of fools." He eyed the small amount of liquid left and quickly drained it before tapping the empty glass on the bar. He looked up at the bartender. "Hit me again, Ralph."

"Are you Patrick D. McBride?"

Patrick swiveled on his bar stool, astonished to find himself facing two tall, burly policemen. His vision was starting to blur, so it took him a moment to recognize one of the men. "You know who I am, Davis," he slurred, his brain grinding to a sudden halt. "What's goin' on?"

"I have a warrant for your arrest," Ted Davis, the older officer, informed him.

"For what?" Patrick asked, taken aback by Davis's formal tone. Patrick had known the man for years, had worked with him on several cases, and they'd shared more than one pitcher of beer together. It would be just like him to see how long he could keep Patrick going about a fake arrest before bursting into laughter. Davis showed no sign of humor.

"Is this some kind of a joke? Because if it is, I'm not in the mood." Patrick swiveled his stool back to face the bar, and his frown deepened when he saw Ralph take his empty glass and drop it into the sudsy water in the sink beneath the bar. Patrick wasn't ready for his supply to be cut off. He hadn't reached the level of total numbness yet.

"Hey, Officer, what's the charge?" Kevin yelled from across the room. Kevin's inquiry was accompanied by the silent but obvious curiosity of the other family members gathered at the table. "Has our Paddy stepped on the wrong side of the law again?"

Patrick winced as he glanced over at the table and noted the amused interest of his family. His parents were whispering to each other. Neal and Kevin were laughing. Tamarra was the only one who looked shocked.

"Don't forget to read him his rights, Davis," Neal hollered. "Otherwise your charges won't stick. We wouldn't want him to get off on a technicality."

Patrick cursed under his breath before snarling, "What the hell is this all about?"

The second officer, Stan Bartlett, a younger version of Ted Davis, pulled out a plastic card from his breast pocket. "Patrick McBride, you have been charged with six counts of contempt. We have been ordered to remand you into custody. You have the right to remain silent—"

"Contempt!" Patrick exploded. "How can that still be on the books? That's a two-week-old charge."

Davis looked at the warrant in his hand and shook his head. "Sorry buddy, these are current charges. This warrant was issued just an hour ago. You'll have to come with us."

Incredulous, Patrick demanded, "You can't be serious."

Neal came up behind Patrick and placed a comforting hand on his shoulder. "Don't worry, little brother." Turning to Davis, he announced, "As this man's attorney, I demand to hear the exact nature of these charges before you take him away."

Davis puffed out his chest as if he'd been waiting for the chance to expound Patrick's alleged crimes. In a stentorian tone, he began, "For disregard of the orders of Judge Blythe Cramer..."

Patrick's brows shot up at the mention of Blythe. What on earth was the woman up to? Was this her way of getting back at him for the things he'd said tonight? He might have lost his temper, delivered a few home truths she didn't like hearing, but as far as he knew, that wasn't a crime.

"For numerous acts of unfaithfulness and disrespect, for contempt for the dignity of the court," Davis continued, undaunted by the stream of expletives muttered by the accused after each charge.

"She has no grounds for these charges!" Patrick declared angrily as the alcohol he'd consumed caught up with him and augmented his bad humor. "What's she trying to prove?"

Neal placed a restraining hand on Patrick's shoulder. "Better keep quiet. Remember anything you say might be held against you. Let's hear him out before we start arguing our case."

It was fortunate that Patrick's mother was too far away to hear his response to Neal's prudent advice.

Davis went on as if unaware of any interruption. "Obstructing the court in the performance of its function, abusive remarks, and..." He paused, pinning Patrick with an accusatory stare that effectively silenced him. "For gross acts of moral turpitude."

"Saints preserve us!" Tom McBride bellowed as he jumped up from the table. "What did you do to that lovely colleen, Patrick? If he abused that sweet lady, Officer, you can throw the book at him. He's no son of mine."

That did it. If there was one thing Patrick knew about his father, it was that in the face of adversity Tom McBride always stood by his family. Blythe had arranged this public humiliation, and his family had been forewarned. He didn't know how she'd accomplished it, but "old snoot face" had gotten the whole bunch of them on her side.

By this time the eyes of every patron in the place were turned on him. If he ever got his hands on Blythe Cramer again, he was going to strangle her. Struggling with his temper and flushed with embarrassment, he addressed the crowd. "This is no big thing, folks. Just a little joke a...ah...friend is playing on me. Please pay no attention."

A man he had never seen before called back, "Moral turpitude can't be dismissed that easily, son. That's the sort of thing that's breaking down the fiber of our community."

Was the whole world in on this stupid joke? Patrick bemoaned silently. At least he assumed it was a joke. It had to be a joke. Blythe was too ethical to bend the law to suit her own purposes...wasn't she? Or had he made her so angry that she'd decided to avenge herself with this public humiliation? *Hell hath no fury like a woman scorned.*

Patrick shook his head, sure he was dreaming. This made no sense. He was the one who'd been scorned. He glared across the room at Kevin, wondering if he weren't the one behind the charges. It would be just like him.

Blythe wouldn't do something like this. She'd be too afraid of the publicity if anyone found out. Her precious public image had always meant more to her than he did. But then again, maybe she did do it. He'd never really crossed her before. She was a passionate woman, maybe she'd finally lost that controlled temper of hers.

Eager to remove himself from further public scrutiny and discover just who was behind this warrant, Patrick said, "Let's discuss this in private, Officer."

Neal negated that suggestion immediately. "No way. These charges are obviously false. My brother has never morally turpituded in his life!" In a stage-whispered aside he asked, "Have you, Paddy?"

"Cut it out, Neal," Patrick ordered. "I don't need you to defend me."

"You sure don't." Kevin shouldered his way to Patrick's side. "I'm much better qualified to plead your case. I specialize in moral turpitude."

At the end of his tether, tired of being the butt of everyone's misplaced sense of humor, Patrick growled, "This has gone on long enough."

"It certainly has," Kevin quickly agreed. "You should have stopped long before committing moral turpitude. Maybe the lady wouldn't be so mad at you."

"Damn you, Kevin." Patrick lunged off the stool, deciding to add assault and battery to the list of charges against him. He reared back his fist, but before he could land a blow, his mother's voice stopped him.

"That will be enough, boys. There'll be no brawling in here. This is a respectable place of business."

Placing herself between Patrick and Kevin, Molly McBride shot a disapproving frown at her third-born. "Go along now, Paddy. As an officer of the court, you shouldn't obstruct these men in the performance of their duty."

"You too, Ma?" Patrick implored dazedly. Even his own mother was against him. He was the wounded party in this travesty but could find no sympathy anywhere. Thrusting out his wrists, he gave up trying. It was Blythe, all right. His mother wouldn't have allowed his brothers to take anything this far. What he couldn't understand was why his mother was going along with things. Maybe the warrant was real.

"Cuff me and take me in, Davis. Let's go by the book. Anything less wouldn't satisfy the judge!" he threw in sarcastically. "'Old snoot face' has always been a stickler for details, you know. Gotta have everything done right."

As the cold metal clamped shut around his wrists, he nodded blearily. "Good job, Davis. The Iron Maiden would have your badge if you didn't hold to the letter of the law."

"Careful, McBride," Bartlett warned. "You're in enough trouble as it is. I wouldn't call the judge any more names if I were you."

Patrick's jaw clamped shut as he was escorted to the door. Before it closed behind him, he overheard his father announce, "This calls for a celebration. Drinks are on the house."

"Has the accused been apprised of the charges brought against him?"

"He has, Your Honor," Ted Davis answered and pushed Patrick forward.

Patrick stumbled across the foyer, blinking in the bright light of Blythe's apartment. This was a kangaroo court if he'd ever seen one. Blythe was wearing her judicial robes and was seated at one end of her dining-room table. A legal-size sheet of paper lay in front of her, along with a copy of the Ohio statutes. Was she going to figuratively or literally throw the book at him?

At least she'd drawn the line at having him thrown in the county jail for a few hours. He supposed he should be thankful for that. He wasn't. "How far are you going to take this, Cramer?"

Blythe hit the table with a rubber spatula. The thud was dull but had the desired effect. Like one of Pavlov's dogs, Patrick responded automatically to the cue and came to attention. "You've not been given permission to address this court, Mr. McBride. Do you have an attorney present to speak on your behalf?"

Through slitted eyes Patrick studied the judge. Snidely he stated, "I prefer to represent myself, *Your Honor*."

"As expected," Blythe decreed. Glancing at the two police officers, she smiled merrily. "You know what they say about an attorney who represents himself."

"He has a fool for a client," Stan Bartlett supplied good-naturedly.

Ted Davis gave Patrick a playful punch. "Sit down, fool."

Holding on to his temper with great difficulty, Patrick slumped onto the chair provided for him at the end of the table. He remained stoically silent as Blythe dismissed the two officers. It wasn't until after they'd gone that he realized he was still firmly cuffed.

"You sure you're not afraid to be alone with me? After all, I'm not totally helpless." He held up his shackled hands. "Your goons made one mistake. They cuffed me with my hands in front. After what you've put me through tonight, I wouldn't be so trusting, if I were you."

Blythe looked across the six feet of gleaming wood that separated her from the man she loved. He was livid. Even knowing that Patrick would never hurt her physically, she decided to keep the cuffs on him for at least a little while longer. Her china cupboard was too close to him, and in his present state she didn't trust that he might not break every crystal goblet he could lay his hands on.

She hadn't expected him to be this furious. She'd counted on his marvelous mind to figure out exactly what she was declaring by this stunt, and his sense of humor should have carried him through any embarrassment she'd caused. Maybe, finally, she'd bested him, but this wasn't the kind of victory she wanted.

"Well, *Your Honor*?" Patrick prompted, jangling the short metal chain between his wrists. "Usually the accused gets to appear in court without shackles."

"This is an unusual case, Mr. McBride," Blythe informed him, striving to stay on the course she'd chosen.

"I'll say," he returned disgruntledly. With a belligerent look on his face, he settled back into his chair and stretched his legs beneath the table. He glanced around the room in a show of boredom and disrespect, his eyes pointedly gliding over everything but Blythe.

Blythe fought hard against the need to run to him, unlock the cuffs, throw herself on his mercy and beg his forgiveness. For once she'd done something unorthodox, ridiculous—she'd taken a very public action—and she was beginning to fear she'd gone too far. However, she was committed now, and she couldn't back off yet.

Patrick McBride needed to be taught an important lesson and shown that he'd gotten himself into this predicament by flying off half-cocked. When she got through with him, she hoped he'd understand the wisdom of listening to both sides of an argument before jumping to conclusions. She crossed her fingers, praying he'd also understand why she'd gone to all this trouble.

Addressing herself to the accused, Blythe began the proceedings. "Mr. McBride, how do you plead to the charges?"

"Not guilty."

Addressing the counsel for the defense, Blythe inquired, "Mr. McBride? Does your client understand the seriousness of his crimes?"

"I don't believe he does, Your Honor," Patrick allowed, his lips twitching. Blythe's actions were the height of absurdity, and he began to understand her purpose, or at least he hoped he did. He didn't know how she was able to keep such a straight face. But if she could, he could. "After all, you said yourself that my client's a fool. Would you care to enlighten him?"

Blythe took heart from Patrick's tongue-in-cheek response. She was making progress. "Very well, counselor. Please advise your client that he would be wise to listen intently."

"I assure you, Your Honor; he's all ears."

Blythe picked up the sheet of paper and began reading from it. "By leaving these chambers earlier today, against my direct order, Mr. McBride showed himself to be in contempt of my office. By refusing to grant the plaintiff, Blythe Cramer, the opportunity to express her great love and admiration for him, Mr. McBride has demonstrated his unfaithfulness and has obstructed the logical conclusion of a beautiful courtship."

"Your Honor?" Patrick interrupted, finding his grin impossible to subdue. He was beginning to feel like a little kid about to dive into his presents on Christmas morning. He straightened his position on the chair as the alcohol-induced fog that had encased his brain rapidly lifted. He was pretty sure he was about to get the best gift he'd ever receive, but knew the joy would be all the greater if he took some time unwrapping it. "My client needs further clarification. Is the plaintiff claiming to love my client?"

"Yes, she is, Mr. McBride," Blythe answered, her blue eyes speaking volumes as they caressed every feature of Patrick's face. "Have you any other questions?"

"Not at this time." Patrick's smile grew a little wider, and his eyes began to take on their usual twinkling lights. "For the present my client and I are satisfied. We're eager to hear the court's explanation of the remaining charges."

Blythe felt the victory shift ownership. When she'd chosen to charge him with five counts of contempt, she'd done it for dramatic emphasis only. It really hadn't been part of her plan that this farcical hearing go on this long. She'd merely wanted to keep Patrick subdued long enough to hear her declare her love for him and for him to understand that if he'd given her the chance a few hours earlier none of this would have been necessary.

By the challenging look on Patrick's face, she was going to have to go the whole nine yards, after all. Taking a deep breath, she continued explaining the charges she'd created. "Ignoring the abusive remarks this court was subjected to, that leaves the most heinous transgression of all."

"Begging the court's indulgence," Patrick interrupted again. "You must be referring to the charge of moral turpitude. My client was particularly confused over what possible action of his could have brought about such an accusation. If it please the court, would Your Honor be so kind as to explain the basis of that charge to him? He was under the impression that the plaintiff rather enjoyed the acts he committed upon her person."

Blythe felt a rush of liquid warmth circulate through her body when she remembered her abandon in Patrick's arms. Clearing her throat, she strove for her most dignified courtroom tone and prayed she'd be able to maintain formal rhetoric. Patrick was doing a good job of it despite his questionable state of sobriety.

According to Kevin, he'd been well on his way to total inebriation by the time the warrant had been served. She'd put on a pot of coffee, but it didn't look as if she was going to have to serve him any. She was sorry she hadn't had a drink or two while she'd been waiting for Patrick's arrival.

"The plaintiff acknowledges that that is true. However, physical acts are not the only basis for such a charge. Base violation of moral principle is also grounds. Mr. McBride is guilty of such violation."

"I object, Your Honor," Patrick stated firmly and jumped up from the table. "My client was never base in his regard or actions toward the plaintiff. I request that the last charge be struck from the record, and that the plaintiff take the stand."

"Objection sustained." After a moment's deliberation, Blythe said, "The plaintiff will take the stand."

Deciding that if Patrick was willing to jump around and pretend to be two people then she could, too, Blythe rose from her place at the "bench" and perched on the corner of the table. She had another ace or two up her sleeve, and it was long past time she played one.

As the counsel for the defense came around the table to address the plaintiff, she crossed one leg over the other, seemingly unaware that her long black robe parted a few inches above her knee and two very shapely legs were revealed. Counsel stopped, leered openly, wolf-whistled audaciously and mumbled about the possibility that his client had been driven to commit moral turpitude.

"Ms. Cramer," Patrick began, coming to stand directly in front of Blythe. "Let me remind you that you are under oath. If you answer my question untruthfully, you will be guilty of perjury. I will ask this question only once. Do you understand?"

"Certainly."

He moved closer, his shackled hands clasped tightly together as he leaned over her. In a low, gentle tone he asked, "Do you, Blythe Florence Cramer, adore, admire, respect and love Patrick McBride to the fullest extent of your being?''

Blythe nodded, so ensnared by the tenderness in his eyes that she completely forgot courtroom procedure. She lifted one hand and curled the palm over Patrick's cheek, while her eyes told him more eloquently than words what she was feeling.

"Visual adoration and fondling are not permissible testimony,'' he warned, but ignored his own warning by turning his face and kissing the palm of her hand. "You must answer yes or no. Do you or do you not love the defendant?''

He lifted his hands and brought them down over Blythe. Caught within a circle of steel and lean muscle, Blythe slithered off the table and stood. Her arms came around his waist, and her hands linked behind his waist. "I do.''

"Do you intend to marry him?''

If Patrick was going to persist along these lines, Blythe was willing to go along. By doing so, one thing was assured. When this "hearing" was over, neither party would have any doubts about the other party's feelings and intentions.

Slipping into her judge character, Blythe stiffened slightly and leaned back as far as the locked handcuffs would allow. "The plaintiff will answer that question after she is assured that the defendant vows to exhibit some patience in all arguments between himself and the plaintiff, and in future, before he forms any conclusion, he will listen closely to any argument she may present.''

A light nudge from Patrick's hands pushed Blythe up against him. Neither judge nor plaintiff chose to keep any distance between counsel and defendant. Their bodies blended.

"My client vows that he has learned his lesson and will attempt to act in a more prudent manner in the future." To seal the vow, Patrick settled his lips over Blythe's so tenderly and sweetly that she had tears glistening in her eyes when he lifted his head. "Now, Ms. Cramer, answer the question. Do you intend to marry my client?"

Blythe gave Patrick a watery smile, and Judge Cramer had to answer on her behalf. "Mr. McBride, Ms. Cramer claims she is unsure of the defendant's intentions and is unwilling to answer your question until she knows exactly what is in his heart."

"Your Honor, my client's intentions toward the plaintiff have always been and will always be honorable. He has adored her since he pulled on her pigtails in the first grade. He has worshipped her since he danced with her in the tenth grade. He has admired her since he shared academic honors at Harvard with her. He fell in love with her when he noticed she wore tennis shoes beneath her judicial robes. From the first moment he kissed her, he couldn't imagine life without her."

Finished with what he thought was as thorough a declaration as was humanly possible, Patrick looked expectantly down at Blythe. "Very eloquent summation, Mr. McBride," she complimented and rose on her toes to add a quick kiss for further proof of her approval. "I, Blythe Cramer, accept Patrick McBride's proposal of marriage."

Sweeping her arms up and around Patrick's neck, she pulled his head down for her kiss. "I love you, Patrick,'' she said against his lips. "With all my heart, and I can't imagine life without you, either.''

"Thank God,'' Patrick said with obvious relief just before their lips met.

There was no more formal or even informal rhetoric for some time. Finally they broke apart for a moment while they both gulped air. Blythe was ready to resume, but Patrick queried, "Your Honor, may the defendant please have his restraints removed. He's about to go crazy with the need to rip that robe off the woman he loves and find out what she's wearing or not wearing.''

Blythe giggled and ducked beneath his arms. Reaching into her pocket, she pulled out the key and quickly unlocked the cuffs. Patrick's hands were barely free before his fingers were busy unhooking her robe.

"And now, who's guilty of moral turpitude?'' he asked with a chuckle as he slipped the robe down the judge's shoulders to reveal the woman beneath. Only a very skimpy, very sheer teddy prevented total nakedness. With a husky groan of appreciation, Patrick swept her up in his arms and started toward her bedroom. "Please tell me you wear more than this in court.''

"Surely you wouldn't think that I, of all people, the Iron Maiden, the very conservative, methodical Judge Cramer would ever be improper?''

"I'm not so sure anymore, Your Honor. You seem to have developed a flair for the improper. Whatever happened to the woman who was terrified of public notoriety? Have you considered what tomorrow's headlines might read?''

"Mmmm,'' Blythe acknowledged as she pressed kisses along Patrick's jaw and down his neck. "Probably will be a real scandal until they get the details of the sentence you're going to get.''

Patrick laid Blythe down on her bed, then quickly shucked his own clothes. Joining her beneath the lacy canopy, he asked, "Just what is my sentence, Your Honor? I don't even recall your verdict."

"It was a strange case," Blythe stated thoughtfully. "Both the plaintiff and the defendant were found guilty of love beyond reason and have hereby been sentenced to life with each other."

"You're a good judge, Blythe Cramer," Patrick declared as he slipped one narrow black strap from a creamy shoulder. "That's exactly the sentence my client deserved."

Silhouette Desire

COMING NEXT MONTH

TOO HOT TO HANDLE—Elizabeth Lowell
Rancher Ethan Reeves quickly exposed his devilish nature to Tory. With his cold eyes and dark presence, she refused to ask him for anything—until she discovered he was really an angel in disguise.

LADY LIBERTY—Naomi Horton
Genevieve needed to protect her grandfather's name by destroying a forgery of the priceless Liberty stamp. But she ran into Griff in the process and found he was a thief—after her heart.

A FAIR BREEZE—Ann Hurley
Leah wasn't interested in involvement—especially in a nosy New England village. But Jonathon Wardwell, the local carpenter, had a plan—and she played a major role.

TO MEET AGAIN—Lass Small
He'd kissed her once, and Laura's marriage hadn't survived the molten memory. Time hadn't extinguished that golden passion, and when Tanner held her, she knew she couldn't leave him again.

BROOKE'S CHANCE—Robin Elliott
A friendly bet landed Brooke on the lap of a department store Santa, and Chance quickly assessed the beauty in his arms. Could she overcome her fears and accept his gift of love?

A WINTER WOMAN—Dixie Browning
Delle's bird-watching college cronies would stop at nothing to find her a man, but she hadn't expected Cyrus, a golden-crested *handimanus hunkus*, who succeeded in setting her soul on fire.

AVAILABLE NOW: